# GWW:2

# The Sad Princess

## John R Parker

# Copyright ©2018 by John R Parker

First Printing: October 2018

Publisher:  John R Parker
eurosphere@hotmail.com

Cover design and artwork by John R Parker
Editorial assistant Clare C Waskett

# Contents

# "Lord, what fools these mortals be!"

A Midsummer Night's Dream, Act one, Scene one - William Shakespeare.

# *Chapter One*

"Alfred."

The weather was unusually mild for late October. Sarah and her young son were taking advantage of this meteorological windfall by enjoying a pleasant stroll in the countryside five miles outside of town. It was two o'clock on Sunday afternoon. The planned hour-long dose of fresh air would leave the lady just enough time to pop into Tesco's before the drive back to their small three bedroom semi-detached house in Lime Lane.

The path that the pair were currently following had been well trodden by the duo, almost since Alfred had first started to walk. In those earlier days, however, the stroll had been undertaken in the company of his late father. They both wished that he was beside them now; it was easy on a fine day like this to believe that he was somehow still there. His wife continued to proudly wear her gold wedding ring, and as yet could not even bear the thought of seeking a new adult companion. Perhaps when her son was a bit older.

It had been a struggle bringing up her child single-handed, a task she had nevertheless managed to perform admirably well. The long hours of hard work brought in enough to get by, yet the worries were ever present. Her own mother provided moral support, even if her age and fragility prevented her from offering much in the way of practical help.

There was a small rustic bridge that crossed a stream where the two ramblers regularly paused to watch the sparkling clean water flow by beneath, staring at the occasional fish that swam slowly past. As they followed this tradition, Alfred could not help remembering the altogether different type of stream that he had travelled upon whilst visiting planet GH34TJ9871CX a mere two months ago. That strange cybotactic river had needed no bridges to cross, and no creatures could live below its surface. What a wonderful thing water was, the earthling thought, appreciating his own world from a perspective that no other member of the human race could possibly possess.

There were very few other people around, just one elderly couple plus a quite young pair of ladies walking a golden Labrador dog. The road they had driven along to get here was some distance away now, meaning that for once there was little audible evidence of the presence of advanced industrial society. The predominant background sounds were the gentle rushing by of the stream, harmonising with the very welcome twittering of various species of birds. There were some cows in a nearby field, and a pretty carpet of wild flowers in an adjacent meadow. This was proper countryside, idyllic, and a shining example of the paradise that Alfred's home planet could be, and really should be.

The pair recommenced their walk, until after twenty more steps Alfred took it upon himself to pause the stroll; he looked up at the clear sky, shielding his eyes from the bright glare of the sun. Sarah copied him, wondering if he was looking at anything in particular. Her son, though, was just briefly pondering what soon lay in store for him beyond the blue shell of the atmosphere.

There had been a short hiatus since his last liaison with anyone from another world, in particular his wonderful furry alien tutor Kriosta. He knew this interlude was to allow a proper plan to be devised for his continued introduction to the marvels of the galaxy. He had received an interstellar text message a couple of days ago stating that things were just about in place, so something, and he had no idea what, was likely to happen very soon. For the moment, as he gazed to the heavens, there was nothing unfamiliar to be seen, only the sky, the occasional cloud, and a handful of soaring birds.

But, fifty miles very directly above the heads of the boy and his doting mother, two monstrously sized heads gazed out through the front windscreen of a jet-black machine from an unimaginably far off domain, watching from an unlit and menacing interior devoid of movement and emotion. The beings stared coldly at the only source of illumination, a small monitor displaying in perfect detail the upturned tiny face of the only earthling to have knowledge of other civilisations well beyond the confines of his home, the magnificent planet Earth. They had found what they had come looking for.

# *Chapter Two*

That evening, the two occupants of the Smith household had been joined by Sarah's mother to share a meal. There was no special occasion to celebrate, it was just a chance for all three of them to share some time together. Sarah had put together a bit of a feast; the three-course meal consisted of vegetable soup with wholemeal bread rolls, spaghetti Bolognese, made with vegetable mince soaked in a delicious pasta sauce, accompanied by warm garlic bread, and for afters homemade rice pudding with a dollop of blackcurrant jam. Truth be told there were a few too many calories, including lots of carbohydrate and sugar, for this tasty repast to be classified as healthy. Sarah had assuaged her guilt by declaring that "It's OK to pig out once in a while."

Alfred was not going to argue the point; he had no complaints about the catering arrangements. Perhaps the only improvement, if he was being unbelievably finicky, would have been the addition of one of the pink bread rolls he had been introduced to on his quest to find the special truffles. He had no idea what the recipe for them was, and in any case he obviously could not make any here even if he could get hold of the ingredients. Their distinctive colour would undoubtedly have led to an extremely awkward line of questioning the moment that his mother laid eyes upon them.

At the end of the meal Sarah, who was sitting with her elbows on the table clasping a half full, or perhaps half empty, cup of coffee looked pensive. She turned to look at Alfred, staring at him for several seconds with a neutral look on her face before it transformed into a smile. "Well, I don't know about anyone else, but I enjoyed that."

"It was delicious Mum, as always."

"Flattery might just get you out of the washing up."

"You're also very beautiful and incredibly wonderful."

Sarah laughed. "I set myself up for that, didn't I? Go on then, you toddle off upstairs for half an hour whilst I clear up. I can see that look in your eyes that says you are desperate to switch on your computer and connect to the internet. But make sure that you are back down in thirty minutes so we can play cards with your Gran."

"Ooh yes, I am looking forward to that," confirmed Alfred's grandmother excitedly. She struggled to cope with the games sometimes, but it was a good way to exercise her aging mind, and she really did enjoy the interaction with her beloved remaining family.

The ten-year-old, now not so far off the grand old age of eleven, got up and pushed his dining room table chair in before heading off with a parting, "See you shortly," prior to bounding energetically up the stairs to his bedroom.

There was a good reason for his haste, since he was keen to deal with an issue that he had been somewhat remiss with, and that he should really have attended to several days ago. Time seemed as ever to be one of the universes most rationed commodities that was invariably in the shortest supply. He could still only afford the briefest excursions out of time, using the time dilator that he had been able to hire from Grinigor's Gadgets, so generally he was just as pushed for precious minutes as the vast majority of the human race.

The specific issue involved sorting out his first official lesson of the online course that he had enrolled upon, at Kriosta's suggestion, for the eye watering cost of seven thousand credits. That included the apparently big discount that he had been offered as the very first human student. However good value it was supposed to be, it had still blown the majority of the credits that he had earned as his share of the profits from the sale of the special truffles. At least the course came with the added bonus of including complimentary periods out of time for the duration of any off-world visits required as part of the course, even earth-bound field trips.

Alfred had wondered if he would age at the normal rate when out of time, but disappointingly the answer had come back that this was so. It seemed there was no such thing as a free lunch anywhere in the universe, or at least anywhere in the galaxy, which was itself an unbelievably huge place.

The CUET sprang to life, reliably as ever, following a short wave of his hand over its egg-shaped top, whirring away like a quiet industrious bee. The monitor atop his desk instantly came alive as he dropped into place on the plain but comfortable enough chair in front of his small wooden desk.

A quick click of the mouse and he was presented with the reassuring two thumbed, seven-digit hand giving him a friendly greeting before dissolving into the home page of the Galactic Wide Web. It felt good to be connected once more to the alien internet.

He intended to contact his tutor to discuss things with him, although that would have to wait until later in the evening. First, he needed to take another look at the notes he had been sent that gave an outline of the course. There were about ten pages of information, although intriguingly much of it had sections labelled TBDL, which he had learnt stood for To Be Disclosed Later. The people running the course, whoever they were, and wherever they were based, had clearly decided that it was not appropriate to apprise the human pupil of too much detail in advance. At least that left an element of surprise and suspense.

Only the first two lessons were particularly expanded upon. Both involved off world visits for two days each. The initial excursion would be to somewhere that Kriosta had previously spoken of with the very greatest reverence. It was none other than the Grand Library itself, the most hallowed location in the entire known cosmos. It was a repository of knowledge in a similar vein to the Great Library at Alexandria in Egypt, one of the seven wonders of the ancient world. That ill-feted building had unfortunately been burnt down, allegedly by Julius Caesar during his visit to meet the beautiful queen Cleopatra. It had been said to house most of the priceless knowledge of the world as it existed before the birth of Christ, and its destruction was arguably the worst act of vandalism plus the greatest material loss in the whole of human history. The Grand Library performed a comparable function, but thankfully was still standing, having survived without calamity since its initial construction well before the dawn of mankind. The alien academic treasure house was protected with powerful security appropriate to its huge importance.

Kriosta, with one of his occasional mischievous and knowing half smiles, had alluded to something during a video chat regarding the Egyptian library that his ward might find rather interesting. There was an implied understatement in his remark, which had had the desired effect of making the earthling really curious, yet what the off-the-cuff comment meant would have to wait for the fullness of time.

The second excursion was to a conservation park on a far-off world. That too sounded exciting, particularly given Alfred's love of nature, plants and animals, however there was no mention of what lay in the park and what creatures it might house. So far, the only unearthly life that he had come across were Kriosta and the kind humanoid aliens he had met on his truffle hunt, along with, of course, the frightening hypercats with their eight legs, big jaws, great speed, and awesome reputation for ferocity. He shuddered at the thought of them, especially how close the duo had come to being torn apart. Frankly he was in no rush to bump into any of them again, even in the controlled environment of a nature park.

There was not too much in the way of preparatory study that was required before setting off on the two field trips. That was just as well since he had his normal schooling to take care of as well. Presumably the people running the on-line course had taken that into account, being careful to make sure that it would not be too demanding.

The preparation for the trip to the Grand Library mainly involved doing some more detailed reading up on the Alexandrian library, along with studying ancient Rome as that city stood at the start of the first century AD, during the reign of the earliest roman emperors. The latter requirement seemed more of a mystery than the first, as its relevance was not obvious. If that was what they wanted though then he would comply; in any case it actually sounded quite an interesting topic.

When these trips would take place was not specified. Hopefully he would get a better idea when he spoke to his tutor after his mum had gone to bed. The fact that the course including an extremely generous allocation of being able to go out of normal time was not just useful but absolutely essential; there would be no other way of being able to disappear off for extended periods. Even so, it was not going to be easy. These were no holiday jaunts, promising to be both quite demanding and tiring. He was also not sure exactly how stressful they might end up being. His first off world excursion had certainly been quite an eye opener, definitely not something for the faint hearted. Such an adventure had really been a bit much for a mere ten-year-old.

As it turned out his desire to contact Kriosta did not work out as planned; rather than the alien's strange yet very friendly face appearing on the screen, there had instead just been a cold plain line of text stating that he was temporarily unavailable, and to try again in two days' time.

"Well," muttered Alfred to himself. "That was disappointing. I wonder where he has gotten to. I hope he is alright."

# Chapter Three

The following day was a school day, so it was back to earth and the more normal side to his existence. Not that normality necessarily meant boring. It was always nice to see his friend Roland, who was always enthusiastic and interesting to talk to. He also enjoyed being in Miss Larsson's class, the beautiful, ever so slightly strange in a very nice Swedish way, teacher from the largest of the great Scandinavian nations.

The school itself, Lime Lane Primary, more commonly referred to as Slime Lane Primary by its pupils, was definitely up there with the best of the state sector educational establishments in the area. It was quite modern and had excellent facilities, including a magnificent indoor swimming pool that was used by many of the less well-equipped schools nearby. The catering facilities for breakfast and lunch were especially impressive by twenty-first century standards, offering a good selection of more traditional school meal fare in addition to the inevitable pizza and chips, the latter being rationed to once a week on health grounds.

Alfred almost never ate breakfast at the school since he was more than adequately fed at home after rising each morning, although he was very pleased that a cheap breakfast was available to any of the other pupils who might not be so fortunate as he was with respect to having such a conscientious parent. He was not on good terms with all the junior attendees of Lime Lane Primary, however he would not have wanted even his enemies to have gone hungry. Maybe the occasional bout of food poisoning to put them in their place, but nobody should be forced to go without adequate nutrition.

The love of all things astronomical was definitely a passion that Alfred shared with Roland. He only wished that he could tell him about the GWW and his off-world visit to look for truffles. That though was completely out of the question, at least for the foreseeable future. If the other inhabitants of the galaxy wanted to make mankind aware of their existence then that was entirely their decision, and for them to do in their own good time. The extraordinary privilege that the ten-year-old boy had been afforded by fate was something that he really appreciated for what it was, both unique and with an implied responsibility to keep the secret to himself.

"Holly, would you be so kind as to bring me the English dictionary from the bookcase."

"Yes, Miss."

Like most people these days from the wonderful country of Sweden, the elegant figure of Miss Larsson was extremely well versed in the language of the smallish country that she had chosen to make her home for the past five years. Clad as ever in pink, today a plain blouse and skirt garnished with a more ostentatious large pink bow neatly gathering her long blonde hair at the back, she had come across a rare word that had caught her out. This was forgivable given the vast number of different words, now in excess of a million, that had accumulated over the centuries within the lexicon of arguably the world's premiere language. Frankly, the majority of the more indigenous population would have struggled to divine its meaning.

"Thank you, Holly. Let me see. Ah, here we are. Perigee. P-E-R-I-G-E-E. Does anyone know what that word means?"

The pupils, all twenty-eight members of Miss Larsson's class, an exactly equal mix of girls and boys, remained silent, looking around at each other to see if any brainbox knew the answer. After a few seconds delay a single hand sheepishly half-rose into the air.

"I might have guessed. Alfred, please tell the class what you think perigee means."

"Please Miss, it refers to the closest point of approach of an orbiting satellite to the body around which it is orbiting."

"My goodness. Excellent. That is almost exactly what the dictionary says. I am very impressed."

The Swedish lady stood up and wrote the unusual technical word out in large blue capital letters on a whiteboard hanging on the wall immediately behind her desk at the head of the class. "There, perigee. Can you all copy that into the back page of your exercise books? It is not a word that I expect you will be using very often, but I think it is a lovely word, and perhaps it will be a good reminder to all of us that we live on a planet, and that there are things called satellites that are constantly circling around our world. Steven, can you tell me what our own planet is called?"

"The Earth, Miss."

"Very good."

The teacher also wrote out the large globe's formal name on the whiteboard. There had been comments by some that Miss Larsson could have had a successful career as a model, however she was a very able teacher whose presence in the profession was something that was much appreciated by pupils, parents and other staff members alike.

She sat back down and surveyed her young audience. "You are all probably wondering why I needed to look that word up in the dictionary. Well, it is because I received a very nice letter from Doctor Brewster at the university congratulating you all on your good behaviour during your visit to the planetarium, and for showing such interest in what you saw. I would also like to add my own thanks to all of you. I was most proud of your behaviour. Give yourselves a round of applause."

The class responded, a touch too enthusiastically, requiring a calming gesture with both hands from the lady in charge. "Thank you, settle down now." Once order had been re-established she focussed her attention in the direction of Alfred, making him wonder if he had done something wrong. "Doctor Brewster went on to say that he had received an email from one of our classmates thanking him for putting on such a wonderful show. That was very polite and thoughtful of you, Alfred."

The entire collective of children turned around to stare at the young author of the email, who was sitting towards the rear of the room. This only enhanced his feeling of having done something not quite right, even if in reality their gazes were purely out of curiosity rather than displeasure. He half smiled, nervously."

"Oh, er, yes Miss. I hope nobody minded me doing that."

"Not at all. When I was a young girl back in my home country of Sweden, it was very common to write thank you letters, especially when one had received a gift. I think that today it is not so common to do that, even though it is actually much easier to do so because people have smart phones and access to email, so I think what you did was a good thing."

Alfred relaxed; he could not help trying to form a mental image of what Miss Larsson might have looked like as a young girl.

"Doctor Brewster used the word perigee because he was telling us about the planet Mars. Apparently, it will soon be as near to the Earth as it will get, and he wanted to invite Alfred to visit him at the university as a thank you for sending the email, where he can take a look at some of the wonderful pictures of Mars taken through the universities telescope. He would also like to present the whole class with a framed print of one of the images to hang on our classroom wall, which Alfred can collect at the end of his visit. Would you like that Alfred?"

The question was rhetorical in the sense that what pupil would turn down such an opportunity, but in Alfred's case the offer was even more welcome as it had far greater implications. This was exactly what he had hoped for.

# *Chapter Four*

"That sounded like a good idea of yours mate, if you really are brave enough to do it. I mean the guy is obviously very smart. Are you not worried about looking a bit dumb in front of him?"

Roland was interspersing his spoken sentences with bites from, and chews on, a Swiss milk chocolate bar, whilst he and Alfred sat on a wooden bench in the main high street of the town centre shopping precinct.

"Well, you may have a valid point there. Yes, it is a little bit of a scary thought, but I really want to do it anyway."

"Any particular reason?"

That was an awkward question that would be impossible to give an honest answer to, and it made Alfred struggle to think of a suitable reply. Close and trusted friend he may be, yet there was no way that Roland could be enlightened as to the real motivation behind his pal's revelation that he had contacted Doctor Brewster at the university in the hope that he could go along for a visit and a chat.

"Well, I er, I…well, it's because I enjoyed the visit to the planetarium so much…actually we all enjoyed the visit so much, that it seemed to be a good gesture on the part of the school to go there and thank him again in person. You know, show him how much it meant to all of us, and how much enthusiasm for astronomy that it has generated."

"I see. Sounds fair to me. But if you are going as the school's representative it's just as well that you cleared it with Miss Larson first. Do things by the book, so to speak. Avoids a lot of aggro further down the line." The munching of the cocoa bar continued apace.

"Well you make another good point. That chocolate is clearly doing your brain a power of good."

It was indeed a good point. Alfred had worded his email to Dr Brewster very carefully, hoping to elicit the invitation that he had subsequently received. But there were other obvious benefits to involving the pretty Swedish lady. For starters, he was going to need some time off school; he would almost certainly have to arrange the visit to take place during a weekday, probably in the afternoon. It was generally difficult to get time off school for anything that was not explicitly medically related, such as a doctor's appointment or trip to the dentist. His tactic made for a much stronger case than just arranging an independent visit for personal reasons.

"Thank you very much for your valued input. You've earned your chocolate bar. Seriously, I owe you a favour."

"No worries mate. Anytime." Roland finished off the last square of the mercifully small sized bar, then he conscientiously got up to walk a few yards over to a nearby litter bin to dispose of the wrapper, before returning to take his place on the bench beside his best friend.

Alfred was grateful to have been blessed with such a good classmate, although he did occasionally worry about the excess weight that Roland carried. Childhood obesity had become something of a national problem in recent years, with a major surge in the numbers affected by the twin demons of a more sedentary lifestyle and copious nutrition. You could not really blame the children, they were no different in evolutionary terms to the previous generation; it was just the changed lifestyle circumstances of the twenty-first century that was the principle culprit, along with an unavoidable genetic factor in some cases.

Hopefully Roland would become more disciplined as he grew older and avoid the heightened risk of developing type 2 diabetes, that modern day plague, in his later years. There was little chance of that fate befalling the galactic web surfer. His mother was quite strict about providing a healthy and generally not too calorific diet for her son, apart from the occasional treat. His decision to become a vegetarian, entirely of his own volition, also helped in this respect, although it had been taken for moral rather than health reasons. Sarah also encouraged him to be active, not always so easy due to his penchant for sitting at his computer. The pair regularly went swimming in the local public pool, in addition to the lessons he received at the school's own impressive water facility.

"Have you thought about what you are going to say to Doctor Brewster when you get there? I guess you will be most interested in the stuff they are doing on Mars at the moment. Who knows, maybe they have found some little green men?"

"Er, yes, indeed, maybe they have."

Alfred tried not to show much emotion in his response, though that was because the not too serious question had in fact touched upon an exceptionally serious matter that had loosely been brought to his attention. Kriosta had mentioned it to him, without giving any further detail. Apparently, there was something about the red planets history that was most important for the young earthling to be apprised of, something that would thrill and amaze him. The typical failure of his tutor to expand upon this had left Alfred a little frustrated and impatient. The boy's subsequent enquiry as to whether it had anything to do with life on Mars had been met with yet another mischievous smile, however no verbal answer. Could it be that life had once walked upon the Martian surface?

# *Chapter Five*

At last Alfred finally had chance to sit down on the rickety chair in front of his rustic desk and make contact with his beloved alien tutor, now that the mysterious sabbatical that Kriosta had gone off on was reportedly over. The absence had turned out to be much longer than originally suggested. Two months was a significant percentage of a ten-year-old's life. It had certainly seemed like a long time. He was missing the furry adventurer, and really looking forward to seeing and speaking to him again.

The youngster waved his right palm across the top of the CUET, causing the faintest of whirring sounds to creep into his ears. As he turned his head back to face the monitor the familiar double thumbed hand came into view to greet him to the Galactic Wide Web.

The hand dissolved to be replaced by the home page, with his personal settings down the left-hand side, along with his account details at the top. He still had a couple of thousand credits left after the recent deduction of seven thousand to pay for his online course. This was, however, no time to be profligate since it would be prudent to keep most in reserve for unexpected costs, or even emergencies. He reckoned though that he could comfortably allow a spend of two hundred credits on things he thought might be useful or interesting, or the occasional small treat that possessed no other justification.

There had been one more addition to his personal shopping mall since first being introduced to Grinigor's Gadgets. It was a clothes shop. The attire on display was mostly decidedly unearthly, both in design and materials used, however it was also possible to purchase terrestrial clothes too. Amazingly, many were styles that were fashionable in eras that had long since passed into the annals of history. Fashion had never been a particular interest of the schoolboy, but this was different, and quite fascinating. One outfit in particular had caught his attention, a very comfortable looking ensemble in predominantly blue hues that looked rather mediaeval, yet also very classy. There was a padded tunic that purported to be resistant to just about everything, fire, water, stains and impact included, whilst being lined on the inside with the softest of breathable fabrics. The trousers offered similar protection and durability. The best bit though, thought Alfred, was a large flowing hooded cloak with enough material to allow it to be wrapped around his whole body to keep him warm in colder climates, and which looked incredibly cool at the same time to boot.

There were some matching accessories, such as a backpack and belt with some useful pouches attached. Frustratingly, the all-inclusive price was an eye watering six thousand credits, so it was out of reach for the moment. In any case, where and when he could possibly have worn it was far from obvious. Certainly not to go to school in!

He optimistically added it to his shopping cart for future reference, although at six grand that could be some way into the future.

Now to the more important business of contacting Kriosta. There was an icon towards the centre of the screen with the alien's miniature image; he double clicked on it just as he would normally have done for more earthbound applications. The screen quickly switched to show a large frozen picture of his intended converse, with the words "please wait" in red spelt out just under his furry chin. Maybe this was an inconvenient moment to call. There was no indication of how long his tutor might be, or what he was up to. Alfred wondered whether he should call back later. Kriosta had said that he would be available this evening in his earlier short written message, however had not specified any time.

Alfred looked behind him at his bedroom door as he suddenly heard his mother's footsteps climbing the stairs. He panicked for a second, thinking she might enter unannounced, although that was not something the respectful lady would normally do. He breathed a sigh of relief as she passed by to her own bedroom, returning downstairs again after a minute.

"Hello".

Alfred whisked his attention back to the screen to see Kriosta's very welcome face, and he could not help smiling broadly with pleasure at finally speaking to him once more. The alien seemed equally pleased at the video reunion.

"Master Alfred. So good see again. So glad."

"Yes, so good to see you again also, sir. How are you, and how did your sabbatical go?"

"Feel good. Good trip. How Master Alfred?"

"I'm very well thank you, sir"

There was a disappointing lack of information about the sabbatical. The earthling was not sure whether that was because his tutor wanted the details to remain confidential, or whether it was due to the alien's poor English skills, plus his general lack of fluency, in talking rather than with the language itself. He did not want to press the issue too much in case it would embarrass his friend, however he decided to make one more hopefully discreet attempt to garner what had transpired.

"You were away for quite a long time, so I hope you enjoyed it and it lived up to your expectations".

"Yes, enjoy much. Learn much."

This was looking like a lost cause, so Alfred decided to let it go for now. Maybe the impersonal virtual communication format was not so conducive to the task of getting a fuller explanation regarding his tutor's travels, and he could try again the next time that they met in person. Which begged the question, when would they be joining up in real space rather than cyberspace? That occasion was almost certainly going to be in relation to the mysterious online course that he had enrolled on at the bequest of his off-world guardians, principally Kriosta, but also representatives from the important sounding Galactic Council that he had been told about. It seemed that the Council existed to administer and control, to a degree, this huge and yet simultaneously small corner of the universe. The scale of the Galaxy and Universe was something that Alfred had in no way been able to come to terms with, particularly the idea of relative size and how something so vast could at the same time be so relatively tiny. For someone who had until only recently been confined to a single planet, which itself seemed enormous enough, it was understandably too much to cope with. The only way to handle the issue was to essentially ignore the problem until such time as his tiny psyche could deal with it, if he ever would be able to that is.

Unsure as to when his mother might return upstairs, Alfred decided to move the conversation forward to the subject of when they could meet up in person once more. "I am really keen to see you again and was wondering how soon that could be arranged. Also, I have been looking through the prospectus for the online course and am keen to get started with that. Maybe we could combine the two with a field trip somewhere? Either here on Earth, or perhaps even visit somewhere else in the galaxy?"

Kriosta looked down and pressed something out of sight using the forefinger of his big right paw. His image was replaced on the screen by a picture of an impressive large building that the young earthling did not recognise and assumed must be located somewhere other than his own world. It looked a beautiful venue, with pretty formal gardens in front of it basking in bright sunshine.

"Wow. What is that place? I don't think I know it."

The aliens head and torso came back into view. "Grand Library. On distant planet, Very old building. Built long before humans lived. Home of online course. We go visit. Soon."

"Really? That is…incredible. Seriously, that is just amazing. I can't wait. I mean, I have been reading about it, and also about the Great Library of Alexandria that used to exist here on earth, which was quite a similar thing. I was hoping that I could go there, so yes, absolutely, I would love to visit it as soon as possible. When can we go, sir?"

The schoolboy was almost unable to contain his obvious enthusiasm, which Kriosta looked very pleased to see, opening his short snout in a smile that clearly displayed the gentle alien's two rows of sharp looking teeth. "Very good. Glad Master Alfred want to go."

There followed an awkward pause, not uncommon during verbal exchanges with his tutor, requiring Alfred to prompt for a piece of information that he felt should have been volunteered anyway. "So, when do you think we might be able to go, sir?"

Still smiling, the absence of an answer persisted, as it seemed Kriosta was not immediately sure what to say. Finally, he worked out a suggested time. "Must speak to Magister of library. Next Wednesday good. Kriosta think."

"Magister?"

"Person head of Grand Library. Great man. Very old. Very wise. Called Magister. Ancient title."

"I very much look forward to meeting him. Although, next Wednesday. That is a school day. Plus, I am going to visit Doctor Brewster at the university next Monday, so that is going to be a busy week. I guess I could still do Wednesday, but there is no way that I could get that day off as well, even if I could think of an excuse."

"No problem."

"No problem?"

"No problem. Go out of time. Not cost credits. Included with course."

"Oh right. I forgot about that. Well I guess it should be alright then. How long will the trip to Grand Library take?"

"Allow two days. Maybe more. Visit other places too."

"Other places. Can you say what these other places are?

"Tell when get there."

It struck Alfred how easily and nonchalantly the trip had been agreed, considering what an incredible and important venture it would be. The mind-boggling nature of what he was involved with was almost beyond comprehension, although this was something that he was starting to grow accustomed to, along with his strategy for coping with it all, which was essentially just to try not to dwell upon it too much. The biggest aid to this tactic was his unerring trust in his tutor.

Kriosta was now no longer smiling, taking on a much more serious expression. "Must warn of two things." Alfred did not say anything, but his own demeanour changed to match the alien's. "First effect of going out of time. Two days not long. Enough though. Master Alfred still age. Be two days older than normal time. Feel very strange next birthday on Earth."

"I think I see what you mean. My real birthday will be two days earlier than my official birthday. My goodness that will, as you say, feel very peculiar."

"Get worse more time spend out of time. Must try limit. Master Alfred say if problem."

"Indeed. Well, let's get the first one out of the way and see how I feel after that, shall we?"

"Much wise."

The suggestion that he should limit the amount of conflict between his real age and his calendar age sounded extremely sensible. Apart from the psychological effect there were undoubtedly more practical issues. Taken to the extreme, it occurred to him that it would be theoretically possible for him to become older than his mother back in normal time!

"You said that there were two things that you had to warn me about. What was the other?"

There was another delay in replying, leading the earthling to worry that this was an even bigger issue than the first. He was to be proved right, as Kriosta seemed to take a deep breath before proceeding. "Many other world's in galaxy. Many other peoples. All think Earth wonderful planet. Not all think humans wonderful people. Some think humans not very good. One race think humans quite bad. Not so good. Problem."

Alfred thought for a moment. "I suppose I can see that we are far from perfect. We certainly have our share of faults. Exactly how big a problem is that?"

"We discuss later. Alfred not worry now. We discuss later."

# *Chapter Six*

"Hello Roland, come on in."

"Thanks mate. Sorry I'm a few minutes late. The twins were pestering me to sort out a problem with their laptop. Got it sorted anyway."

"Hello Roland. Come on in. Would you like a cup of coffee? How are your parents?" Sarah always made a bit of a fuss of Alfred's best friend when he came to visit. She very much appreciated his friendship for her only son.

"Oh, thanks Mrs Smith, a coffee would be brilliant. Milk and three sugars please. My folks are fine, thank you."

"Coming right up." There was a tiny squint of disapproval accompanying Sarah's hospitable smile regarding the request for the third spoonful of sweetener, but it was only born of genuine concern at the youngster's burgeoning waistline.

The two boys wandered over to the sofa of the living area of number fifty-three Lime Lane and settled onto its comfortable cushions. Sarah switched off the television before heading off into the kitchen, correctly assuming the soap opera it had been showing would be of no interest to the ten-year-old budding scientists.

"Did you get the answer to that homework question, mate? Bit of a stinker I thought."

"Er, yes, it was not obvious. Bit sneaky really. Most unlike Miss Larsson to be so mischievous."

"So, the answer was Einstein then?"

"Er, nope. It was Niels Bohr."

"What? Oh man, my dad said that it was Einstein. Are you sure, oh wait, of course you are sure. Damn. That's what you get for asking a bank manager about the history of physics. I'll have to change it when I get back. Just as well I've got you to put me back on the straight and narrow. Well, you and the world wide web."

Alfred squirmed a little in his seat, knowing that his friend was not a hundred percent correct regarding his host's use of the internet, specifically the added opportunity to benefit from the information stored within the unimaginably vast Galactic Wide Web.

"As you say, I can only claim a little credit. The internet really is a wonderful thing."

Sarah reappeared, carrying a small round tray with two pale blue mugs of coffee freshly poured from the filter machine in the kitchen. It smelt delicious, the real thing, brewed from a choice blend; it was not cheap, but represented one of the few luxuries that the hard-up lady always insisted on buying.

"Here you are, boys. Go careful, it's still quite hot." She put the cups on the coffee table sitting in front of the sofa and then stood up, folding her arms across her body after giving her slightly tangled yet still pretty hair a quick flick to send it cascading behind her shoulders. "It really is nice to see you, Roland. How are you getting on at school?"

"Oh, not too bad, Mrs Smith. We are very lucky to be in Miss Larsson's class. And Alfred put's me back on the right path when my dad gets my science homework wrong."

"Oh dear. Well, he has a successful job at the bank. I guess most of us can't be good at everything."

"What about you, Mrs Smith? Did you have a favourite subject at school?"

"Me? Well, I did use to like history. However, I was not very good at maths or science, so I am very certain that Alfred gets his science brains from his late father, bless him."

"I like history too. Do you have a favourite period?"

"Ooh, that's a good question. I suppose that I would love to be able to go back in time and visit ancient Egypt. You know, the see the Pyramids and the Sphinx in their heyday. Ooh, and visit the Great Library in Alexandria before it got burnt down."

Alfred had just started sipping from his mug when the unexpected revelation made him gasp and nearly choke on a mouth full of the hot liquid going down the wrong way. His mother looked over with a worried expression as he quickly put down his cup and began coughing uncontrollably.

"Excuse me, mum," he managed to splutter.

"Alfred, dear, are you alright?"

"Sorry, forgot not to breath and drink at the same time."

Roland gently patted him on the back. "Take it easy mate. Don't choke, I need you to help me with my science homework."

Alfred managed a smile as he began to recover. He took out a tissue from his right pocket to wipe his mouth. "I didn't know you were such a Pharaoh fan. Interesting," he said, finally regaining his composure. "We got some homework on that subject this week."

Roland looked surprised, and almost shouted with more than a hint of panic, "Did we? I don't remember that. When are we supposed to hand it in?"

Alfred suddenly realised to his annoyance that he had inadvertently mixed up his schoolwork with the reading task that he had been given as part of the online course on the GWW. He understood that such confusion was bound to happen occasionally, however that made it no less embarrassing when it did occur, and he struggled to retrieve the situation.

"Oh, er, no, my apologies. Sorry Roland, we don't have any history homework to do. I got confused with something else."

"Really Alfred," scolded Sarah, not too seriously. "You nearly gave poor Roland a heart attack. What on earth did you get confused with?"

The recently enrolled student of the alien educational course had noticed in the past that his wonderful mother had an uncanny ability to ask really awkward and probing questions about all manner of potentially incriminating things that concerned the unfortunate youngster, accompanying such inquiries with an unintentionally ruthless stare that the head of the Spanish Inquisition would have been proud of.

There was no legitimate answer, at least none that he could possibly give, so it was once more time to just bluff his way out as best he could. "Well, er, it was just something that I came across at random on the internet, completely by coincidence. I believe it was a newspaper article on the subject."

"Oh, that's interesting. I wouldn't mind reading the article myself. What newspaper was it?"

The problem with bluffing is that if you are not careful you can end up just digging yourself into a deeper and deeper hole.

"Oh, er, sorry mum but I forget. Really sorry. But if I suddenly remember then I will definitely pass the information on to you."

"Oh, that is a pity. It did sound interesting. You know it's about time I relit the fires of my interest in ancient Egypt. Maybe you could have a look on that CUET thing of yours to see if there are any good books on the subject. It is not long until my next birthday, so maybe you could get one of them as a present for me."

"CUET?" "What's that?" asked Roland, unfortunately latching onto the unusual word like a crocodile snapping its jaws around a tasty meal that had inadvertently strayed into its territory. This conversation was not going Alfred's way. The last thing he wanted was for anyone else to get wind of the alien device.

"Oh, it's nothing really. It was a mail order catalogue that some company sent me. There is a section with some books in it, maybe there is a history section in it. I will take a look later."

Sarah looked puzzled at the less than accurate response from her son. She did not know much about the strange, ostensibly simple computer; however, she certainly knew that the CUET was more than just a glossy paper catalogue that Alfred had speculatively been sent. Thankfully, the lady seemed to sense that he did not want to elaborate further on the matter and stayed silent. She did give her son one of her something is not quite right here looks though, which Alfred timidly did his best to ignore by staring down at the small table and then taking a diversionary gulp of coffee. He managed to drink it this time without further mishap.

# Chapter Seven

The university was technically not part of the town that Alfred lived in but belonged instead to the nearby city. In practice, however, the main campus lay outside the confines of the larger conurbation and fortunately on the right side to be so close to the town that it was physically barely half a mile away. It was only a twenty-minute ride from the bus stop fifty metres away from the front door of number fifty-three Lime Lane to the main entrance of the physics building. According to the university's website the faculty was blessed with a large and attractive five storey dwelling with a basement that housed a particularly swish enhanced café that was good enough to almost be classed as a proper restaurant, save for the self-service requirement.

Alfred was just grateful that he had been given the afternoon off to make this journey as he sat five rows back from the bus driver. He had frankly been very surprised at how little resistance there had been from the school following the submission of his unusual request. The direct intervention of Doctor Brewster had clearly done much to smooth the potentially choppy waters, aided somewhat by the thinly disguised crush that Miss Larsson obviously had on the handsome lecturer.

The bus was fairly full, mostly of old age pensioners making the trip to the shops of the high street in the city centre. The availability of free bus passes, combined with a relative lack of retail establishments in the small town, meant that the route was always popular with the veterans amongst the local population. On-line shopping was also less popular with this more elderly age bracket, who were naturally less comfortable about purchasing things from the internet, and probably less trusting of the World Wide Web. Alfred wondered how they would feel about using the Galactic version of the internet.

He had still made only a few off-world purchases so far, yet felt completely happy to do so, except for the need to exercise caution with respect to his mother's awareness of what he was doing and buying. There was no question of ordering goods that were too large to be easily hidden away in his bedroom, or so clearly alien in origin as to give the game away. Fortunately, he did not have to worry about that too much at present since he simply did not have sufficient spare funds, after deducting the cost of his education, to buy many items. That would presumably change with the passage of time as he accumulated additional credits, however that was tomorrow's problem.

There was little thinking time available during the short journey, but one issue that he did wrestle with was what Kriosta had said about not all alien races being happy to leave the human race to its own devices because of the bad things that it was doing to its own planet. His tutor had not laboured the point, however the lack of detail inevitably opened up the door to all sorts of speculation and concern. Could it really be that the earth's dominant species, in its arrogance in believing that it could not be threatened by any other civilisations, was in fact setting itself up for its own demise at the hands of an as yet unknown, but in reality far more powerful race of beings.

Again, that was tomorrow's problem, albeit a potentially nearer tomorrow.

Alfred tried to put these thoughts out of his mind as his stop drew near, prompting him to press the closest button requesting the driver to pull over and open the doors. The university campus was not huge by modern standards; there were only two stops, the first of which was usefully right outside the physics building. As he alighted there were only twenty paces to the ten steps that led up to the main entrance. He paused briefly to look over the large structure, managing to feel simultaneously humble yet just a little self-important as well. He justified the latter emotion by virtue of the fact that he appreciated as much as anyone the importance of education, and this was his very first visit to a university, which he was doing at the tender age of ten.

There were several actual students entering and leaving as he climbed the steps and walked in, but only one, a young lady, reacted to his obvious youth, peering at him with an inquisitive gaze followed by a polite smile.

At last he found himself inside his destination. The man behind the reception desk in the foyer of the physics building looked down with an expression that clearly said that he did not know why the ten-year-old schoolboy was cluttering the area immediately in front of his enclosure. He stood leaning on folded arms without speaking, as though hoping that the unwelcome lad would leave of his own accord.

Alfred stared upwards, also without speaking, like a lost child helplessly waiting for his mother to come and collect him. The normally articulated youngster had temporarily lost all confidence, in awe of where he was and what he was doing.

The man continued to wait passively and sternly. Finally, it became clear that his unwanted visitor was not going to budge, and he stood up straight, looking as irritated as he could manage.

"Can I help you?"

Alfred was just able to give a croaky voiced reply. "Yes, sir. If you please. I have come to visit Doctor Brewster. I have an appointment with him at twelve o'clock."

The man looked unconvinced. "Really? Are you a relative of his?"

"No, sir. I am a pupil at Lime Lane Primary School."

That did not really explain the incursion, but it was enough for the receptionist to feel obliged to contact his academic colleague, so he slowly lifted a telephone handset from the counter, all the while keeping a beady eye on the unusual stranger.

"Ah, hello, sorry to trouble you, sir, but I have someone here at reception who says he has an appointment to see you. His name is…"

The man's face switched to an inquisitive expression, courtesy of which he received an obliging "Alfred Smith, sir."

"Alfred Smith. He says he is a pupil from Lime Lane Primary. Oh, I see. Very well, I shall tell, er, Mister Smith that you are on your way." Still appearing perplexed, but now a little bit more receptive, the receptionist managed a trace of a smile. "Doctor Brewster will be along to greet you shortly."

"Thank you, sir."

A couple of young women, presumably students, arrived at the counter and engaged the official in their own conversation, so Alfred stood to one side and waited patiently for his host to turn up.

He surveyed the lobby during the short hiatus, fascinated at how completely different this educational establishment was to the one that he was used to. There were of course no other children, no school uniforms, and additionally it was not clear cut who were the teachers and who were the students amongst the visible population of about twenty people. Even the older members of the throng could well have been more mature students, which he knew was not uncommon these days. Perhaps in long past semesters the lecturers might have plied their trade wearing distinctive gowns and caps, but there was no place for such formality in this very modern tertiary school.

As it turned out the message given to him by the man was not quite accurate; it was a young woman who eventually appeared from the right hand of two nearby lifts and made a beeline for the visitor, her raised heels clattering over the tiled floor. When she arrived, she held out her hand expectantly, which Alfred eventually grasped and shook lightly, his hesitation clearly a result of not being used to the more adult etiquette.

"Good to see you, Alfred. My name is Heather, and I am one of the post graduate students here. If you would like to come with me, please, I will take you straight up to Roger's office."

"Thank you very much."

With that she turned and resumed the clattering for the return journey, this time via the left-hand lift. Doctor Brewster's office was on the third floor, midway along the building. Heather knocked politely on the open door of the office and then left.

"Hello. You must be Alfred. Yes, I am sure I remember that handsome young face. Welcome to the physics faculty. It is so nice to see you again. I think you must qualify for the title of our youngest ever visitor. Please take a seat."

"Hello, sir. It is a great pleasure to see you again. Thank you very much for inviting me."

Doctor Brewster's office was not very big, and there were only two chairs available, each occupying one side of medium sized desk that was cluttered with several piles of paperwork. Alfred complied with the hospitable request and sat down. It felt a rather intimidating place to be, even if the senior academic was doing his best to make his very young guest feel at ease.

There were two tall grey filing cabinets set against the left wall, each housing four drawers. To the right the room boundary was bordered by two high bookcases, and nearest the door a small whiteboard decorated with a multi-coloured array of incomprehensible equations that were way beyond the grasp of a mere primary level mathematician. It made about as much sense as if it had been written in Chinese.

Brewster was wearing a fairly casual outfit of light buff trousers, white shirt, woollen jacket of a light green hue, and dark green tie, similar to what he had worn at the planetarium. It all sort of matched, and seemed to suit his character. His slim frame, youthful early middle age looks, and neatly quaffed golden hair made him unquestionably attractive, so it was no surprise that Miss Larsson had seemed to take a bit of a shine to him.

The lecturer removed his jacket and hung it on a hook on the left wall near to the window at the back of the office, and then he too sat down in a plush executive chair that seemed to be the only sign of opulence in the modest room. He then leant forward resting with his arms folded beneath his torso on the only small part of the wood laminate's surface that remained free of stationary.

"We will pop down to the café in the basement for some lunch shortly. And don't worry about being a vegetarian because I am too, and the good news is that there are quite a few decent options for us. A lot of people believe that the café is the best thing about our building, but I like to think that we do quite a lot of interesting work too." He rummaged through some of the papers in the smallest pile and extracted a single sheet. "I spoke briefly to your teacher Miss Larsson by phone earlier, and she confirmed to me what I already expected, that you are very interested in all things to do with space and astronomy. Personally, I got the same bug when I was about your age, and I think it is great that you find it fascinating too."

"Definitely, sir". His enthusiasm for the subject had been with him for as long as he could remember, though it had obviously been enhanced somewhat in recent months.

"Excellent. Is there anything to do with space that particularly interests you? I seem to recall you asking a very good question at the planetarium about whether life exists anywhere else in the universe?"

"Er, yes, I believe I did." It had of course been a rhetorical question that the schoolboy most unusually already knew the answer to, and had been asked solely to get the academic's opinion on the matter. Alfred knew that he had to tread very carefully with his words so that he gave no clue regarding his own certainty about the existence of alien lifeforms. "I guess I was really keen to find out what an expert like you thought, as opposed to all the programs I have seen on television about the possibility of alien beings from other worlds having visited us."

Doctor Brewster laughed. "Yes, I have seen a lot of those programs myself, but I don't remember ever being convinced by any of them. They are certainly good entertainment, although I personally do not believe we have received any visits from little green men in flying saucers." Part of Alfred was bursting to correct him, but that was certainly impossible, at least for now. He fully understood the lecturer's reply though, since the clever man had not had the benefit of stumbling upon the GWW as he had. "However, I am firmly convinced that life in some shape or form does exist somewhere in the universe. If not in our own galaxy, then certainly elsewhere. The universe is simply too big a place for that not to be true."

"I agree, sir. I mean I don't understand anywhere near as much as you do, but it just seems ridiculous that we should be the only planet where life has been created."

"Good. And thank you for the compliment. You may be young and inexperienced, but you have clearly got a lot of brain cells in that little head of yours."

"Thank you also very much for that compliment. The other thing to do with space that really interests me is the planet Mars. I guess because it is so close to us, but also because it is the only planet in the solar system that seems like it might have had life on it in the past."

"Well, as I think you know, the planet Mars is one of the specialities of the department here. Being honest, a big reason for that is my own personal fascination with the Red Planet. I am so pleased that you seem to be a fan of the place too. I am definitely starting to like you, young man."

Alfred blushed a little yet was happy that the two seemed to be hitting it off so well. That was very important to him. He was overjoyed with having stumbled on the Galactic Wide Web and thrilled that it had led to him meeting aliens and visiting a far-off world. However, he also felt incredibly isolated in a way, since he was the only human being who possessed that knowledge. However friendly his extra-terrestrial acquaintances had been, it still was not easy to be going it alone, especially given his very young age. Perhaps he harboured a subconscious hope that in time he may be allowed to share his secret with another human, and the good doctor seemed a perfect candidate for that. For now, it was very reassuring to at least be able to talk with someone who knew so much about space, the solar system, and even the galaxy.

"Anyway, shall we go and continue this fascinating discussion with the aid of some delicious food in our restaurant? Our treat of course."

"That would be wonderful, sir."

# *Chapter Eight*

"This is interesting." Alfred had a tendency to whisper to himself whilst engrossed in surfing the internet, terrestrial or otherwise. The object of his immediate fascination was an online Wikipedia article, plus its extensive references and further links, regarding the Great Library at Alexandria in ancient Egypt. It was built during the early part of the Ptolemaic dynasty, the last of the old family reigns of the pharaohs that ran for three hundred years ending in the year 30 BC. The founder of the dynasty was King Ptolemy, who had been one of Alexander the great's generals during that astonishing man's conquest of the bulk of the known world at that time.

The final ruler of the dynasty had been Queen Cleopatra. Alfred, like pretty much everyone else of his age and above on the planet, had of course heard of her before. What he had not previously realised was the fact that she was the seventh female leader of the nation to bear that title. The legendary demise of Cleopatra VII at the hand, or rather the bite of, an asp was as famous as the saga of her ill feted romances with both Julius Caesar and Marcus Antonius. It had been during the Queen's tenure as ruler of Egypt that the library had unfortunately caught fire and been burnt to the ground, with the loss of its priceless literary treasures, running to hundreds of thousands of scrolls and books.

The library, at its peak, was more than just a repository for the written word. It was part of a larger centre for knowledge, education and research called the Musaeum of Alexandria. There were works of art, sculptures, lecture theatres, rooms in which to meet and talk, and beautiful gardens to stroll in and just think. Many of the finest minds of the day would make the arduous long journey to the library, long before the availability of mechanically aided motion, which served as a magnet for philosophers, writers and artists alike. Notable amongst such visitors were the luminaries Archimedes and Euclid.

Kriosta had informed his young pupil that it would be extremely useful to study the background to the Egyptian library, since there were remarkably close parallels between it and the distant alien Grand Library, even though there was no actual historical link whatsoever. The similarities were the principle reason that the subject had been added as one of the first major elements of the curriculum of his online course on the Galactic Wide Web. The people who ran the Grand Library were apparently big fans of the now defunct earthbound version. Representatives had even taken clandestine trips to Earth to study its history. There were experts dedicated to the investigation who had travelled across the Middle Eastern country to various archaeological locations, where they had pored over the large number of relics and architectural remains that still exist even up to the present.

Intriguingly, the researchers based at the alien establishment had developed a wondrous tool that gave them the ability to study ancient Egypt in even greater detail, however Kriosta had refused to give any more information about that. Even more thought-provoking was the fact that Alfred's tutor had alluded to a consequent discovery, made quite recently, which related directly to the destruction of the Ptolemaic Great Library. Frustratingly, what this discovery had been was also classified as something that must remain a closely guarded secret for now.

The trip out of time to visit the Grand Library had been scheduled to take place just two days from now, so there was little more opportunity left for preparation. Apart from his Egyptian studies there was not much else he felt he could do. The reluctance to apprise him of much detail about what would be happening once he got there, understandable though this was, meant that he could do no more than take some bare essentials in a small bag and then wait to see what transpired. Kriosta had told him not to worry about anything, but that was much easier said than done. The sheer enormity of the venture, coupled with his natural uncertainty about how well he would cope with it, and how he would be judged by all the advanced aliens that he would shortly be exposed to, it all made him extremely nervous about the journey.

Despite the apprehension, he was undeniably also excited. Frankly, there were so many conflicting emotions flowing through his small body that he felt like it might be in danger of just exploding. He returned his attention to the article on the screen, gazing at an artist's impression of the magnificent Great Library, hardly able to accept that soon he would be looking at the Grand Library for real.

# *Chapter Nine*

As the roundabout that served as the normal rendezvous point for his excursions with his tutor came into sight, Alfred stared hard, but could see absolutely no trace of the spaceship. It was, as usual, a grey day weather-wise. It had refrained from raining, at least since he had got out of bed that morning, which helped with concealing the invisible vehicle.

Having just gone ten o'clock, the Wednesday rush hour traffic had dwindled to a couple of cars a minute, with a similar trickle of pedestrians. Normally he would have been at school, but today was a very fortunately timed inset day where the teachers were undergoing training, so Lime Lane primary was temporarily closed to its pupils.

These occasional interruptions to the curriculum were generally welcomed by the children, but Alfred was particularly grateful today; it had afforded him an easier opportunity to once more team up with his wonderful alien tutor and go for a ride in his ramshackle yet likeable spacecraft. Serendipitously, the inset day had presented the perfect opportunity to make the first official field trip of his online course, fittingly to its headquarters based within the precincts of the famous Grand Library.

It had been three months since there last physical meeting, so Alfred was really looking forward to seeing his furry friend in person again. To celebrate the occasion, he had brought along a little present in the shape of a large four-hundred-gram bar of premium Swiss milk chocolate. The treat had not been cheap, however he felt that the money had been well spent, especially after observing just how much the alien had enjoyed the earth sourced confectionary during their adventure on planet GH34TJ9871CX. In truth, Alfred was looking forward to sampling a few squares of the blend of cocoa butter and sugar himself.

The lack of traffic made it no problem to cross the road to the large grassy island, but he then paused since he was not quite sure what to do next. He assumed that Kriosta was monitoring his approach from inside the bulbous rocket, although could obviously not be certain about that. So, he just stood a little awkwardly waiting for something to happen.

This impasse continued for fully a minute, to the point where the young boy was beginning to wonder if perhaps there had been some mix up over the time of the appointment, or maybe if there had been some issue that had delayed his tutor. He turned around as a car with an unpleasantly noisy sound system passed by immediately behind him, but as it sped past it suddenly came to a complete stop, accompanied by a merciful muting of the annoying music. It was an eerie effect, but he knew at once what had caused it. Returning his gaze to the traffic island, he was overjoyed to see the smiling face of Kriosta standing in the open main entrance to his spaceship. Alfred could not help smiling back broadly as he walked forward to climb inside.

"Hello. It is terrific to see you in person again. You are looking very well. Permission to come on board, sir."

"So good. Love see Master Alfred again. Please enter."

The alien took one pace backwards to let his young passenger in, helping him negotiate the high step by then leaning forward and giving a gentle tug on the small earthling's upper arms.

The main cabin seemed pretty much as when Alfred had last left it, however it was definitely a little tidier, as though the pilot must have made an effort to give it a spring clean. The pair headed straight through to the small cockpit where the alien took his rightful place in the left-hand pilot's seat, as befitted his status as captain. The novice interplanetary astronaut was more than happy to be allowed to sit in the comfy right-hand seat, where he dutifully strapped himself in.

Kriosta reached his right paw over to the central part of the control panel and pressed a blue button. The outside world began to move again as time returned to normal. The spaceship was now completely invisible again, so there was no need to be out of time. With time being such an expensive commodity to manipulate, it was important to be as economical with it as possible, even if the people organising his course were paying, indeed especially as they were being so generous in footing the bill.

After fiddling about adjusting a few more switches and controls, Kriosta sat back in his chair and the strange craft began to slowly move upwards, beginning its ascent into low earth orbit, the first phase of their journey to the stars. After five minutes they were comfortably above the possible flight paths of any commercial airliners or military aircraft, so the experienced pilot pressed forward one of the two main small joysticks positioned by his right arm to begin accelerating in the forward direction as they continued their climb. The atmosphere began to rapidly darken, and before long they were hurtling around the globe at nearly eighteen thousand miles an hour at a height of just under three hundred miles.

As an added bonus to the astonishing feeling, Alfred noticed the gleaming structure of the magnificent International Space Station in the distance not so far away, certainly near enough to be able to make out a fair amount of detail. It would have been nice to have given the occupants a wave as they flew past, and that would definitely have made the cosmopolitan crew's day a lot more interesting, however there was no way such a greeting would have been allowable. He gave them a wave anyway, even though he knew they could not see him

Having achieved the initial goal of cruising around the blue planet in a lowish orbit, Kriosta switched on the gravity compensation system so that they could undo their harnesses and move freely about without ending up floating awkwardly around the interior of the vessel. He then moved off into the main cabin without speaking. Alfred assumed that his tutor must want him to follow, although he was actually quite absorbed by the extraordinary view beneath, which he could happily have continued to look at for another hour. He knew that this was no sightseeing trip though, so reluctantly unstrapped himself and wandered through to the largest room of the spaceship, where he saw Kriosta sat waiting for him in one of the two chairs positioned on opposite sides of the low table in the middle of the cabin. He took the other seat and stared expectantly at the alien.

"Wanted tell about library planet. Far off. Take lot of power get there. Take some time. Fully charge engine first."

"I understand. Can you put a figure on the distance?"

"No point. Very far. Other side of galaxy all Alfred need know. Very, very far."

"Fair enough." The curious schoolboy would not have objected to being given a number anyway, but he got the message that it was not local. His limited knowledge of astronomy told him that it should take an unimaginably long time, far longer than his own lifespan, to make the trans-galactic journey. Fortunately, they had the services of the peculiar device that served as the main engine, if you could call it an engine, of the spacecraft. The technology was unfathomable to his primitive human brain, and he only barely grasped the principle point that it somehow made use of the weird area of physics known as quantum mechanics, a subject well known to many scientists on earth yet not that well comprehended even by the best of them. It was the closest thing to magic in the rigorous world of science, and arguably more unbelievable than any illusion pulled by the cleverest of professional magicians.

"Three important worlds should know. Also planet Joxavia, not discuss now. First Grand Library planet. Second conservation planet. Third we call Olympus. Like Greek gods of Earth history. No gods there. We visit Grand Library planet first. Kriosta favourite place. Think Alfred like too."

"Well, I have studied some of the known facts about the Great Library in Egypt as part of my course, and I found that very fascinating, which is a good sign. It may technically be homework, but I must say it does not feel like a chore. It's all a bit different to school, that's for sure."

"When reach planet we land, meet students. Beautiful place. Go meet staff. Visit library contents. Then meet important people. Want meet Alfred. Talk Alfred, important things. Must warn, serious things. May be difficult."

"Oh?" said Alfred, a little surprised and unsure about what his tutor meant. "That sounds a little worrying."

"Alfred not worry. Good people."

"O-kay." The youngster slurred the acknowledgement, not wholly convinced by his tutor's reassurance. He was really looking forward to visiting the library, but he was not sure that he was one hundred percent looking forward to that meeting.

# Chapter Ten

There was something unnerving about going into orbit around the planet where the Grand Library was located. The excitement of visiting the repository of all the knowledge of the known universe was at the moment tempered by the perceptible fear of hurtling around what seemed to be a giant black hole. It was not completely black, but a very dark and dirty shade of grey that made it visible at this close a range, yet there was no chance of such tiny intensity of light ever making it as far back as the Earth some forty thousand light years away; certainly not with enough strength to be detected by any human observers. Even the mighty Hubble telescope would not be able to see it.

There were no features whatsoever visible on the planet's surface at this height, and Kriosta explained why this was, since there was supposed to be a large city surrounding the library.

"Planet have two atmospheres. Inner, outer. Inner like Earth's. Much oxygen. Outer less dense, very thick. Lot dust. Little light in. Little light out."

"Well that explains the darkness, but how do people see if there is no sunlight? And doesn't it get really cold?"

"Artificial light. Fusion plants. Heat and light. Still night and day. All controlled."

"Amazing. Are the two atmospheres a natural phenomenon or was it engineered that way?"

"Bit both. Natural. But enhanced."

"I see. Did they choose this planet for the library for that very reason? I mean to keep it concealed?"

"One reason. Built long time ago. Very old. Change much over time. Ancient and new. You see soon."

Kriosta fiddled with the controls, and his passenger suddenly felt being thrown forward in his harness as the spaceship slowed and began a careful descent. Alfred was still very much a novice astronaut, however he was beginning to get accustomed to both the procedure plus the unusual feeling that came with the deorbiting process for planets with an atmosphere. This was not going to be anything like as intense as astronauts back on earth experienced, such as in the Space Shuttle or Soyuz capsule, since this spaceship used a powered descent to control the rate of aero braking. It took longer to move downwards through the atmospheric particles, so slowed more gradually, and consequently did not heat up so much. Nor were the forces on the occupants so severe. It was noticeable, but not particularly uncomfortable.

The controlled fall was a bit like going down through the white clouds during their return to earth from the trip to search for truffles, but here the clouds were very different due to the griminess. It took nearly thirty minutes before they finally emerged into the much clearer inner layer of air, and what a magnificent sight it was that eventually came into view. By now the pace of their forward motion was quite moderate; they were approaching a large city some two miles away directly ahead of them and about a mile beneath the present altitude of the spaceship. It was broad daylight, and seemed like a beautiful summer's day with little apparent cloud cover in the inner atmosphere. There was of course no real sunlight, yet Alfred marvelled at how natural the scene looked. There was no sense of the area being floodlit.

The approach and descent continued, allowing the earthling to get an improving picture of the city. The biggest surprise was that it lay on the shore of a vast sea over which they were still flying. The water was a beautiful blue. Whilst this was in one way expected, as water was kind of supposed to be blue, Alfred's alert mind realised that perhaps it should not look blue since the sky here was completely different to that back on his home planet. He made a note in a small pocket book that he had brought along for the express purpose of jotting down questions that he could find the answers to when convenient.

"This is sensational," blurted out Alfred, unable to control his enthusiasm.

"Yes. Wonderful planet. All love come here."

As the shore bordering the city came ever nearer Alfred spotted a huge building directly ahead of them. He did not need to ask his tutor what it was, as it could surely not have been anything but the Grand Library itself. Whilst still not close enough to pick out every detail, one thing that was obvious, apart from its size, was a large golden dome with a short spire jutting out above its apex. This topped off a very wide but not so deep structure, predominantly white, and perhaps ten storeys high. It sat close to the shoreline, with about a hundred metres of garden in front stretching down to a substantial seawall, and a small golden beach in front of this.

There were some tiny boats on the water, and to the left about a mile away was a small harbour with two larger ships moored, one of which was a sailing ship, whilst the other astonishingly looked quite ancient, like an ancient Greek trireme. That was intriguing, to say the least.

As the bulbous spaceship reached the shore and then swept over the high dome of the central part of the Grand Library, another magnificent sight came into view at the rear of the building. Stretching out for perhaps a mile was a fabulous landscaped garden with a multitude of areas that were variously adorned with flowers, shrubs, trees, outbuildings and water features. The artificial sunlight sparkled off the surface of a small lake as dazzlingly beautifully as it had done off the ocean. There were birds clearly visible in the trees and floating on the patches of water, looking remarkably similar to those on earth, indeed so similar that Alfred wondered if maybe they had been imported.

There was a narrow stream that ran parallel to the library not far from the white stone rear facade, or perhaps it was even marble. Several small bridges crossed the liquid obstacle, including a rather grand silver bridge located on what appeared to be the main path leading through the gardens from the library.

Immediately behind the building was a large terrace where quite a few people were sitting at tables. Kriosta guided his beloved spacecraft a little way over the cultivated space whilst progressively slowing down, before then turning through one hundred and eighty degrees and heading back to the terrace whilst simultaneously descending. Finally, he touched down about thirty metres away.

By now many of those seated had stood up and begun to walk towards the spaceship to form a sizeable welcoming committee. It was becoming obvious that they had been expecting the arrival of the freshly landed vessel, and in particular its cargo of the very first human being to visit the ancient and venerable site.

The expectant throng had unfortunately completely spooked the young arrival from Earth. The sense of occasion was palpable, a bit too palpable for someone in no way used to being so much the centre of attention. As mobs went this was an extremely friendly looking bunch of assorted species, the majority quite humanoid, but with several that were clearly more exotically formed and deviating from the standard smooth skin, two arms and two legs specification. One comforting sight was a member of the alien audience with purple hair that Alfred recognised as surely a resident of the planet Norros, where Grinigor's gadgets was based. Could it be that he was even related to the wonderful Grinigor himself?

Kriosta unstrapped his large frame and looked over at the nervous student sat in the right-hand seat. "We here." Alfred was very much aware of that fact as he tried not to tremble with trepidation. "We get out. Meet other students"

There was no choice but to comply with the instruction, so Alfred undid his harness and followed his tutor through to the main door of the spacecraft, covering the short distance on rather wobbly little legs.

There was a loud cheer as the two appeared in the doorway of Kriosta's characterful vessel, making Alfred simultaneously pleased and embarrassed. As they jumped down the crowd applauded, then parted to allow the visitors through. The air was warm, still, and felt extremely fresh and unpolluted as the youngster gratefully grabbed a huge lungful after the extended trip from Earth. The weather matched the best of summer's days back home, helping to make him feel a bit more relaxed. He was not really sure how to respond to the generous welcome, so just smiled, waved and called out, "Thank you all very much. You are most kind. I am honoured to be here."

Kriosta copied his wave as he led the duo through the enthusiastic multitude towards the magnificent library building, whose rear had a great many windows that no doubt afforded good views over the spectacular gardens. As a place to work and study this could surely have few equals. Alfred could not think of anything to match it in his previous, albeit limited, experience; for a moment he wondered how it would have compared to the original Great Library of Alexandria. It at least surely shared the same supreme spirit of the absolute importance of knowledge and learning.

The pair climbed a series of ten long steps to ascend onto the large main terrace, then continued through two open glass doors into the prestigious building. A large hall with a pure white marble floor lay immediately inside the rear entrance to the library. In the middle were two sweeping staircases that both led up to a gallery on the next floor that ran in a square all around the room, and which overlooked the ground floor. The bottoms of these wide stairs were separated by a few yards. They both had curving black metal rails fixed along their length, and royal blue carpets covering the steps.

Just behind the stairs on the ground floor was a long bronze table with a dozen stout legs supporting a thick table top. There were two long wooden benches either side that could each seat perhaps twenty people at a pinch, and at each end were placed substantial carver chairs, although it did not give the impression of being a dining table, rather something for more administrative purposes.

At present there was nobody on their current level, a little surprising considering the large number of beings who had been gathered outside. There were however several bodies looking down from the balustrades of the gallery, and a single person standing waiting at the top of the right-hand stairs. He was dressed in white robes, was quite heavily built, and had short greying hair.

Kriosta pointed up towards the distinguished looking figure. "That great man. That Magister. So wise. We go meet."

"Magister? I recall you using that word before, and it sounds like something I should know, but I don't really remember."

"Senior person at Grand Library. Great man."

His tutor obviously held the Magister in very high regard. "I really am quite nervous, but looking forward to meeting him at the same time. Shall we go up and greet him?"

Kriosta waited for his pupil to go first, following just behind. It was a peculiar sensation walking up the stairs, the journey taking some time and spent in eerie silence. The Magister seemed emotionless and statuesque, not scary, yet quite intimidating given his position and elevated status. His hooded full-length robes made him appear almost religious, like the abbot of a monastery. Indeed, this whole place had the ambience of a cathedral as much as a place of learning. Maybe in the grand scheme of things the search for meaning and the search for knowledge shared a common ultimate goal.

The visitors stopped three stairs below the Magister, who bowed his head slightly to acknowledge their presence. "Welcome to the Grand Library, my friends. My name is Grattin, and it is my privilege to bear the honorary title of Magister of this great institution. It is wonderful to see you again, noble Kriosta, but may I particularly welcome you, Master Alfred Smith of the planet Earth. This is an historic moment, and we are all overjoyed to have you here with us today."

It was a warm and kind salutation that left Alfred feeling very humble and grateful. The head of the library still looked intimidating, however it was clear that he was a wise, friendly and gentle man of huge intellect.

"Thank you, sir. May I say what an honour it is to be here. This is a magnificent place. And may I also thank everybody involved in organising the online course that I am so lucky to have had the chance to enrol on. I am just so excited. I only hope that my little human brain can manage to cope with it."

Kriosta moved up to the top step and placed both paws on the shoulder of the Magister. It was obvious that they already knew each other very well. "So good see Grattin again. So good."

At his tutor's beckoning Alfred joined them on the gallery level. He glanced around to gaze at and admire a regular line of white marble statues than ran along the walls in both directions. The subjects were a mixture of humanoid plus less recognisable creatures. Surprisingly, some seemed to be antique artefacts from his own planet, and there was a painting on the wall nearby that looked remarkably like something that Leonardo de Vinci might have painted. Could it really have been fashioned by that famous artistic maestro himself?

"Would you both please follow me? My chambers are nearby, where you can freshen up, and we can take some refreshment."

The offer was welcome after their long journey, although the phrase long journey almost had no meaning. Back on earth a trip to London would have been a long journey. The countless billions of miles that they had recently covered was beyond the schoolboy's capacity to comprehend, to the point where he simply avoided thinking about it.

The Magister's private quarters were entered via a door in the corner opposite the stairs they had ascended. The first room was in fact a large office, with an imposing dark wooden desk that sat in front of a panoramic window that looked out over the front aspect of the library, giving a magnificent view over the front gardens down to the seashore and out over the beautiful sparkling blue ocean. There was a big sofa and a couple of comfortable chairs on the visitor side of the desk, whilst on the other side was an enormous cream padded chair for the Magister to sit upon.

Moving through this space they then entered an inner apartment area, the first room of which was a smallish yet extremely plush and comfortable looking lounge. In one corner was a dining table with eight place settings, upon which sat an array of crockery, utensils and cups, along with assorted containers of food and drink. The Magister led them to this and gestured to them to sit down. Standing by the table was a young blonde-haired gentleman dressed in a simple blue tunic who seemed to be some sort of steward since he began to pour a juice type liquid into three waiting glasses.

Kriosta gratefully gulped down an entire glassful in one go, looking thirsty and very grateful for the quenching offering. The steward refilled his, and then began to dish out a salad-based meal along with a large dollop of something that resembled an Indian korma dish with chunks of presumably vegetable protein material.

"Please help yourselves. I hope you find it palatable," said the Magister, taking a seat along with his own helping of the meal.

"Thank you," replied the two visitors in unison. The salad and alien korma turned out to be more than palatable, and they consumed it with gusto.

"Once you have eaten we will rest for a few minutes, and then I will take you down to the library itself," advised Grattin.

"Down to the library?" asked Alfred, a little puzzled. "I thought that this was the library."

"Well, technically it is part of the library, but what you have been able to see so far is more the academic building where much of the teaching takes place, and where we hold meetings and public lectures. The main part of the library, including the vast repository of books and knowledge, is contained within the main vaults which are situated beneath the gardens at the rear of the building. In fact, there are forty subterranean floors divided into different levels according to origin and subject".

"Wow. That is almost unbelievable. I think that it might take a while for me to work my way through that lot!"

The Magister smiled. "Well, indeed it might. Of course, it is impossible for even the staff to have a complete knowledge of everything that we have here. The collection has been built up over many millions of your years and comes from all corners of the galaxy. I often find myself being surprised, if not astonished, by completely new things that researchers and visitors managed to find in some far-flung part of the lower levels. Who knows what wonderful secrets remain buried in plain sight down there? At the very least it does make my job more exciting."

"That is truly astonishing. It did not occur to me that you would not be aware of everything, but when you explain it I guess that makes perfect sense. What about you, sir? Do you come to visit the library quite often?" Alfred had turned his head towards his tutor to pose the question.

"Yes. Kriosta love Grand Library."

"I would say that is an understatement," interjected the Magister. "Kriosta has been one of our most frequent patrons over the last few centuries. I sometimes think that he knows more about what is contained in the vaults than I do. There must certainly be an enormous amount of knowledge packed into that modest yet very clever brain of his."

Alfred patted his tutor on the shoulder, and with a big grin said, "I always thought you were a genius, sir."

The furry alien looked embarrassed and took another gulp of juice. Alfred patted him again, more slowly and sincerely.

"Anyway, make yourselves at home and have a short rest," invited Grattin. "Soon I will take you down to the repository. We take security very seriously here, and so the vaults are reached through a short tunnel with enormous, thick doors that can be closed in the unlikely event that there is some issue that requires such an action. You will understand that this is a very, very, very important place and so we have a duty to take care of it. One more thing that I must stress, although I think that you are already notionally aware of this; there is much that you are not allowed to be made aware of at this time, and as a consequence there are certain areas of the library that are strictly off limits to you. Other than that, you will be free to roam about at will. Once again, Master Alfred, welcome to the Grand Library."

# *Chapter Eleven*

Walking along the dimly lit tunnel that led to the subterranean vaults was an emotion filled journey that left Alfred feeling undeniably fazed, yet bursting with anticipation. Being the very first human being to visit the Grand Library was a great honour, although he could not ignore the thought that he did not personally deserve that accolade. After all, who was he other than a nobody school child from a small English town that most people on his own planet had never heard of? It had been pure luck that he had accidently stumbled upon the Galactic Wide Web. At least it was almost certainly merely good luck. The amazing events of the last few months had opened his eyes to all sorts of wonders and possibilities, and that had left him with a revised mind-set that often left him wondering if he could be certain about anything anymore. Perhaps there was something more proactive at work than mere chance. Who knew?

The fact that he was a little apprehensive was born of the significance of what he was about to do, as well as that insignificance of his own identity and ego. The hallowed vaults of the library that lay ahead reputedly contained all the known information of the galaxy since time immemorial, and a great deal of it would likely be way beyond his own experience, intellect, and probably even imagination.

The excitement was born of the same reasoning though. How could he not be excited at the prospect of getting access to the incredible repository of knowledge from the far reaches of this particular segment of the cosmos?

Actually, he was now very aware of the fact that his access would be strictly controlled due to a variety of reasons, not least for the sake of his own sanity. It was not going to be a cakewalk dealing with it all from a psychological perspective. Kriosta in particular had been careful to emphasise the need to take his exposure to all things galactic at a gentle pace for the boy's own wellbeing. The other main reason for controlling what he could be exposed to was for security purposes. It was not, they had been keen to emphasise, that they did not trust the earthling; it was a simple matter of procedure. Much of the knowledge was classed as beyond what the human race as a whole could be exposed to or trusted with. Alfred thought that such rules were fair enough, especially as he invariably did not trust the human race as a whole either.

There had been two gigantic metal doors at the start of the tunnel, and he could see ahead another set of identical barriers. There were no visible guards, but he sensed that there were many additional security measures in place here even if he could not see them.

The tunnel had been accessed by a set of stairs further along in the left-hand wing of the educational building that spiralled down in a broad helix leading to a spacious basement area where the tunnel commenced. As they neared the second set of security doors to their collective left was an entrance to a very big service elevator, with the doors open but nothing currently inside. Two much smaller personnel elevators stood on either side of this.

Kriosta and Grattin flanked the earthling as they arrived at the end of the tunnel, where it gave entry to a large open reception room with several desks manned by a mixture of young men and women uniformly attired in the same simple tunic that the steward had worn, but this time all coloured yellow. They looked very human, with the exception of rather larger heads than would have been found on earth, but not large enough to appear in any way freakish. Instead it just made them all appear quite intelligent.

Alfred noticed, as they passed through the stout metal inner doors, that painted on the otherwise cream solid floor there was a short zone where it changed to a dark blue shade. Upon entering this the two aliens suddenly stopped, and his tutor put a paw in front of the youngster to gently arrest his progress too. They then waited without speaking for a few seconds, until a brief flash of pale blue light completely engulfed all three for about two seconds, before evaporating as quickly as it had appeared. Kriosta and Grattin then moved forward again heading towards the nearest of the desks.

"Excuse me, sirs, what was that light for?" asked Alfred.

Kriosta was first to reply. "Security scan. Record details. Match with database. Check we safe let in."

"What if we were not safe?"

"Sound alarm. Not be able move. Guards come."

"I see. I'm glad it approved of us."

The trio were greeted by a female member of staff, who looked no older than a teenager, and who rose from her chair as a gesture of respect at the sight of the approach of the Magister. To Alfred's surprise the two began a brief conversation in a strange language that was completely incomprehensible to him. He was so used to the aliens that he had thus far encountered speaking almost perfect English, admittedly somewhat broken English in the case of Kriosta, that it came as quite a shock to hear them speaking in such a peculiar extra-terrestrial tongue. It was a useful reminder, if one was needed, that he was far from his home world.

Kriosta began to smile, as though he understood perfectly well what the other two were saying, but did not join in the conversation himself.

"Eventually they ended their short discussion, and the young lady bowed her head with a pleasant smile and spoke to her even younger visitor in perfect modern Anglo Saxon. "Welcome, Master Alfred. I hope you enjoy your first journey into the vaults of the Grand Library. And I also hope that this is merely the first of a great many visits here."

"Thank you so much, Miss. I hope so too."

"What you see before you is the main reception to the library," announced the Magister. We have hundreds of wonderful staff that help look after our treasures of knowledge here. Most of them are dispersed elsewhere throughout the various levels, but you will find them all very friendly, very knowledgeable, and very helpful. Many of them are students here at the library, on courses like yourself. Many are graduates who work as full-time researchers on all manner of interesting and important subjects. Others are conservationists and archivers who work on cataloguing particularly the older and more esoteric works."

Grattin wandered further into the middle of the reception space, followed by his guests, before continuing. "The monitors you see around you at the various desks can be used to make enquiries and searches. The screens are touch sensitive and programmed to respond in all known galactic languages, including English of course!"

"Very useful," commented Alfred. "May I ask how many different languages there are?"

"Unfortunately, I cannot tell you that, even though I do know. Sorry, but I hope you understand, or at least accept the position that I must take."

"Of course, sir. No problem. I hope you do not mind that I asked."

"Not at all. Please feel free to ask any question you like whenever you like. It is unlikely that anyone will ever take offence, just do not be surprised if people are sometimes obliged to politely decline to answer. Anyway, let me take you through to show you one of our collections of books. If we go down to level three you will be pleased to see that a large part of that floor is dedicated to entries from Earth."

Passing through reception and out of a door on the far side led into a narrow corridor that eventually opened out into a very large square room with a high ceiling. Dominating the centre of the room was basically a gigantic square hole with an enormous wide staircase descending down into its hidden depths. The trio walked to the top of the stairs allowing them to see down into the hole, which turned out to appear almost bottomless, winding round in a square spiral cascade of endless sections of fifteen steps per side. Around the edges of their current floor were several open entrances to lifts that gave easier access to the lower levels, as well as large maps on the walls showing the layout and contents of each level. Judging by the size and quantity of these maps the area of the galleries on each level was vast, perhaps not so surprising when taking into consideration just what a big place the galaxy was. It made it very clear that the number and variety of alien civilisations must be beyond the wildest dreams of anybody back on earth. No wonder Grattin had said that there was so much information here that the administrators could not possibly be aware of what it all was.

"If you don't mind we shall take the stairs down to level three as it is not so far to go. We can come back up in one of the elevators," suggested the Magister.

That seemed reasonable, so Alfred nodded in agreement. He had already surmised that the gravitational attraction on this world was a little less than that on Earth anyway, making it easier to move about and making him feel slightly fitter than he really was. Not so fit as to decline the kind offer of using the lift for the return journey though.

The wide stairs had glossy black railings and white slabs for the steps that looked like marble but were not nearly so hard, firm but not harsh to walk down. As they wound round the second step they could see that the next level, the first one down, looked identical to the top one, except for having a different set of maps that corresponded to the layout of the books and other exhibits for this section. Something that caught Alfred's eye was that the maps had seemed to change perceptibly just as they had come into view. Grattin seemed to anticipate his curiosity about this and explained the effect. "The maps on each floor are not actual paper pictures but are made from an extremely thin polymer that acts as a video screen. I have a little gadget in my pocket which transmits my personal details and profile, and the receiver behind each screen picks this up and switches the information to display in the corresponding language. If there are several people who each speak a different language, then each screen uses a setting appropriate for whoever is nearest to it at any given time to avoid conflict. As you can see I have set my gadget to English for your benefit. Before we exit the vaults, we will formally register you, and you will get your own transmitter for your personal use in the future."

"Wow, thank you. What a clever system."

It did not take long until they found themselves staring at the various maps of the third level, and Grattin directed his youngest guest to a sidewall that was dominated by entries from the planet Earth. There were certainly a lot of them, covering a substantial part of the entire floor.

"Anything in particular take your fancy, Alfred?"

"Er, well, I don't know. There is just so much of it. I really don't know where to start."

The Magister laughed. "Don't worry. You'll have plenty of time in the coming years to explore everything, or perhaps not everything, but still a great deal of what we have. Why don't we just go in and briefly wander around to give you a flavour of the collection."

"Sounds good to me, sir."

"Alfred watch." Kriosta moved along to an adjacent map, having so far stood well back, and Alfred could see that particular screen suddenly change to a different setting. Grattin remained where he was whilst the youngster went to take a closer look. The language displayed was now definitely not English, with very peculiar characters replacing those he was naturally familiar with. Interestingly, the letters were generally in different colours. His tutor grinned proudly. "This Kriosta native language. Much complex. Much different to English. Colours of letters change meaning of words. What Master Alfred think."

Well, I don't understand a single word, of course, but it looks very beautiful. I'm afraid that I am pretty hopeless when it comes to learning other languages, although maybe you could teach me a little sometime."

Grattin now moved to join them, and Kriosta took a few steps back. Sure enough the screen flickered back to English, and Alfred could not help laughing with delight at the wonderful technology. "Come on young man, let us go inside."

The Magister led the way round the corner to a large pale green door set in the next sidewall. As they drew near its two halves slid apart to reveal a truly remarkable sight. The room inside had a main aisle directly ahead that seemed to go on forever into the far distance, with row after row of bookshelves branching off on either side. The young earthling had been told that the library was big, but he was not prepared for this. The reality turned out to be so far beyond what he had imagined that he could not help letting out a loud gasp. And this was just one floor of the library.

"Unbelievable. This place is HUGE! It is just magnificent."

# *Chapter Twelve*

"The what? I mean, the who?"

"The Joxavian race. They are really the only species in the known galaxy who could be described as aggressive. Not exactly war mongering, but they do not suffer fools gladly."

It was something of a surprise to learn that not every advanced civilisation in the galaxy was as docile as those that Alfred had so far come across. Grattin presumably had some further agenda behind this revelation, and the earthling was keen to discover what this was.

"Excuse me, sir, but am I likely to come across these people in the near future?"

"Possibly, but more to the point is the ongoing risk that the human race as a whole might come to interface with them before long."

"Really? I thought that the Earth was more or less to be left alone to its own devices for the time being."

"Well, that is the general principal that most races adhere to, however the Joxavians are inclined to a very different point of view. Their opinion is that the destruction of the Earth's natural environment by the human race has already gone far beyond what can be tolerated and allowed. To be honest, they are not entirely without support from many other citizens of the galaxy. I am sorry to have to say it, but there is very great disquiet regarding the situation on your planet right throughout the cosmos."

Alfred fell silent for a moment. He shared the alarm regarding the behaviour of his own species, and he felt ashamed, even though he was sure that had not been the intention of the alien academic. At the moment he was sitting on one of the large visitor's chairs in Grattin's spacious office on the first floor of the Grand Library. Kriosta, at the Magister's request, was not present but instead sitting in the lounge of Grattin's private quarters. The earthling had just been treated to a pot of very nice Jesepian tea, a local brew, perhaps to calm him down before the start of this uncomfortable discussion. He had, in truth, harboured a nervousness from very early on in his galactic adventures that there must be those who might pose a threat to the completely dominant species of his own world.

"I'm sorry to worry you, but I felt it best that you should know."

"Thank you for telling me, and yes, I am worried. Are the Joxavians going to invade the Earth? If so, what might they do to the people there?"

It was a very blunt question. Grattin tried his best to ease his student's fears. "Nothing will happen for now. The Joxavians are very powerful, but they would be reluctant to take any immediate action that was clearly opposed by the Galactic Council. One can never be certain about such things though, and at least in the medium term there is certainly a serious risk of some sort of intervention."

"Could there actually be a war between the human race and the Joxavians?"

Grattin's face took on a troubled expression. "With respect, Alfred, it would not be a war as you might imagine it. The difference in technological development is enormous. Humanity could not hope to defend itself against such a formidable military power. The only question about the outcome would be what punitive measures would be taken against your fellow people."

"Do you mean that the human race could be wiped out?"

"Highly unlikely. Understand that the Joxavians are not a bad civilisation. Any intervention would take place solely to protect the other species on your planet, and not for the benefit of the invaders. By that same token they would not wish to exterminate humanity, but they may consider that they have no choice but to instigate a cull of the population, rather like humans themselves have been known to do when certain indigenous fauna have experienced uncontrolled expansion to the point where they pose a serious threat to the local environment. Rats, for example."

This was truly shocking news; the analogy comparing humans to rats was not entirely appreciated, however valid the argument. Alfred hung his head in his hands, prompting Grattin to try to do something to comfort the boy. "More tea?" he asked, meaning well, but the gesture seemed a little trivial at the moment. Alfred looked up and thought, yet could think of nothing to say. He nodded his head, and moved his large, almost bowl sized cup near to where the Magister was sitting at his desk.

Grattin filled the cup from a huge teapot of the sort that might have hung over an open fire back in the Victorian era. He then stood up and wandered round to join the earthling, sitting down on the adjacent visitor's chair. There was no milk, as was the normal practice here, but on the other hand there was also no need for the dairy addition since the tea tasted quite delicious anyway.

The beverage was still at a perfect temperature, which the pot seemed to control without any obvious means of doing so. The student gulped down a couple of mouthfuls whilst clamping the cool outside of the cup between both hands and ignoring the handle.

"It seems to me, sir," said Alfred, trying to be constructive, "That it is unlikely that things are going to change back on Earth, and that if anything it is going to get worse as the population continues to expand. Would it not be possible to do something else other than killing lots of people? Could the world leaders not be contacted to discuss the problem with them?"

The Magister reached over the desk and dragged his own cup over to take a brief drink before answering. "There are several things that could be done, in theory, but they would each involve outside interference. That is very much something that all advanced races do not like doing. If it comes to a choice between just letting the Joxavians go ahead with a cull though, or interfering in some other way, then there may be no choice left but to go for the latter option. That is where you may end up being involved yourself."

"Me? With respect, sir, how could I possibly become involved?

"Well, actually your accidental discovery of the Galactic Wide Web has, perhaps unfortunately in one sense, led to placing you in something of an awkward situation. As the only representative of your species who possesses knowledge of the existence of other life throughout the galaxy, by default you are the only human that we can ask to get involved at this time."

"You mean that I have dropped myself in it?"

Grattin took another sip of tea. "A very colloquial English expression, but perhaps a very good way of putting it. I should stress that you do not have to get involved. You have, and always will have, an absolute right not to do anything. From the little that I already know of you, however, I suspect that you will not exercise that right. It would actually be a big help to us to have you involved."

Alfred took a particularly big gulp of the tea. "What do I have to do, sir?"

"The first thing is to have a formal meeting with the Galactic Council."

"The what?"

"It is a small yet very important and influential group of representatives of all the races within our own galaxy. I am sorry to spring this upon you at such short notice, but they are actually here at the Grand Library now, and if you are willing, then I would be grateful if you would agree to appear before them in about an hour."

The schoolboy's heart skipped a beat at the invitation to the completely unexpected appointment. This did not sound like a fun occasion. "I do want to help, but it sounds quite frightening. Will Kriosta be able to come along to support me?"

"I am really sorry about this, but on this occasion, no. There are strict procedures that we must abide by. I really am sorry, but it is not an option."

"Very well, I agree."

The Magister gave him a look that seemed to be one of both gratitude and admiration. "We can go and join your tutor again now for a while, then I will have you escorted to a waiting room in the right wing of the upper library in preparation for the meeting."

The slightly jaded earthling took a final sip of the dregs of his cup of the calming Jesepian tea. Right now, he felt as though he would need to consume the entire contents of the large pot in order to even begin to calm his jangled nerves.

# *Chapter Thirteen*

The waiting room turned out to be ultra-Spartan; it was one of the last places that anyone would want to wait in for any length of time at all. It would have served perfectly as a police interrogation room, placing guests at considerable unease and discomfort, as well as inducing a sense of foreboding. Alfred felt all three sensations as he sat on a single hard plastic chair, resting his chin atop arms fixed on the only other piece of furniture in the small room, a medium sized table constructed from what back on earth one would have assumed to be oak.

There were no windows. A clinical pure white light from the ceiling bounced off equally clinical pure white walls. Even the hard-plastic floor was the same harsh non-shade. It was sufficient to strain the eyes and force them half shut. Neither was the room particularly warm.

The minutes passed in near silence, except for a very slight low frequency hum that might have gone unnoticed were it not for the complete absence of anything else to stimulate the brain.

Alfred had developed some anxiety about this significant day even before breakfast back on Earth, which had grown during the journey; this inhospitable delay was greatly amplifying his nervousness and not helping at all. It was true that half of him felt excited about the unique opportunity that he had been given, however the other half was a rather timid ten-year-old boy who wondered exactly what it was that he had let himself in for. The burden of being effectively an ambassador for both his planet and his species weighed heavily upon his young shoulders.

What on earth was keeping his hosts? He grimaced, then managed a half smile as he realised the inappropriateness of that particular question here, but it barely broke the tension.

Frustration took over as the dominant emotion, prompting Alfred to rummage in his right-hand coat pocket for his mobile phone, before remembering that he had been asked not to bring it, so it was currently languishing in the cabin of his tutor's spaceship. He rolled his eyes in mild disgust, then sat back with his arms now off the table and instead folded in front of his chest.

Doing his level best not to get annoyed he reflected on the fact that he was clearly not the Tibetan monk type; forced solitude and inactivity did not sit well with his character. This actually came as something of a surprise, since he had not previously considered himself as the impatient sort. In mitigation he was a child of the twenty-first century, where the normal plethora of electronic devices and other things to look at or fiddle with were enough to sap the attention span of even the most meditational of youthful psyches.

At last there was a click of the door lock, which opened to reveal a figure clothed in bright scarlet robes with a full red hood that so completely covered the head that no face could be seen. It entered just enough to be able to stand to one side of the door with an outstretched hand that signalled a clear invitation for Alfred to exit the room despite the lack of any verbal instructions.

Alfred slowly rose from his plastic chair and, resigned to whatever lay in store, walked meekly past the attendant and out into the corridor, before pausing and waiting for his chaperone to emerge and lead the way. He almost felt like a condemned prisoner waiting to enter a court room to hear the verdict of the jury in a murder trial.

After twenty measured metres, the corridor turned sharply to the right to end in six steps that fell towards an arched black door. The attendant turned a brass knob and pushed the door widely open, then passed through. On the other side was a short sunken corridor that quickly met a further six steps going upwards this time. He did not climb the steps but allowed his charge to go on alone. Alfred ascended the stairs and found himself inside a cavernous theatre like chamber with about fifty rows of tiered seating formed in a semicircle around a raised rectangular stage. Placed towards the rear of the stage was a wide table covered by a two-tone cloth, the far half being pure white, and the nearer half jet black.

On the other side of the table sat nine assorted individuals, so different in appearance as to be obviously from a variety of planets and species. Occupying the middle and grandest seat, slightly raised above the others, was the Magister of the Grand Library. The only other person that the earthling recognised was the big, rotund Mayor of the planet, physically dominating the less massive remaining members of the seriously demeanoured panel. He had not met the mayor, but there had been a small framed photograph identifying him on the wall of Grattin's office.

The tunnel had emerged towards the front of the seating just below the left-hand side of the stage. There was a single plain seat placed on the black side of the table in the middle directly opposite the Magister. It did not take a genius to work out that this was where they intended him to sit, so Alfred headed for it by climbing onto the stage via some steps located at the left side of the stage. He paused by the chair, thinking it would be impolite to sit down before being invited to do so.

"Please sit down, Alfred," obliged the Magister. "This must seem very unfair of us to place you in this unpleasant situation, and I apologise for doing so, but it is very, very important that we have this formal meeting.

"I don't understand any of this, sir, but I do want to help to make things better. If my being here is of any use then I am willing to participate. But I am quite scared."

"I thank you, and I personally guarantee that you will come to no harm."

The Magister turned to his left before continuing. "I would like to introduce my fellow Galactic Council members. The two gentlemen nearest to me are both senior academic researchers here at the library. The lady next to them is president of the Federation of Small Planets. The gentleman at the end is the Mayor of this great planet, who is also responsible for security matters on his world." The Magister now turned to his right. "These other four committee members are all administrative heads from the largest four civilisations in our galaxy. As such they are very influential regarding what goes on in this part of the universe."

The two researchers wore robes similar to those of the Magister, but coloured dark grey, and they both looked rather older. The four world leaders were an assorted bunch. Two of them were quite humanoid, one with very dark skin and the other very short in stature like a midget back on earth. The other two were markedly different. One had a much larger head with two enormous eyes and a short beak, almost octopus like, and had a cylindrical body with four tentacles in place of arms and hands. It was the most unusual looking species that Alfred had thus far come upon during his travels, and it was hard for him not to stare at the creature. The final committee member on that side, whilst of broadly human construction, had a rough, green, almost reptilian skin.

The only female member of the panel was the elegant president of the Federation of Small Planets, and her own planet of origin was given away by her beautiful long purple hair, making her unmistakeably from Norros.

What the diverse panel stretched out before him must have thought of Alfred was hard to say. The diminutive earthling was not the most domineering of sights or personalities. How much they appreciated just how young he was remained unclear. Strangely enough, Alfred had not met anyone during his off-world jaunts who could really be described as a fellow child. Even Eltora was hardly an infant, more a young adult. She came across as being in her mid to late teens, although he had never inquired after her age; for all he knew she could have been a hundred years old. He secretly hoped that she wasn't and instead really was literally a teenager.

The Magister's calm but authoritative voice brought the schoolboy's attention back to the task in hand. "The purpose of this meeting is to formally give you notice that the human race is now officially classified as a severe threat to the other indigenous species of the planet Earth, and to its natural environment in general."

Alfred felt the words tear through him like a knife going through butter, especially coming from the hitherto very kind and respectful head of the Grand Library. He gulped and did not know how to respond.

The Magister, having made the blunt statement, looked quite distressed himself at what he had been obliged to say. "I am very sorry that you are in the very awkward situation that we have put you in, however my motive is to ultimately help your species. The laws, such as they are, that apply to the galaxy as a whole have certain specific formal demands and procedures that I, especially, as Magister must adhere to. That proclamation is part of the process required to try and deal with the alarming situation on your home planet. Without such a proclamation initiating the relevant process then the door would have been left wide open for individual races within the galaxy to act unilaterally. Can you understand what I am trying to say, Master Alfred?"

The precisely crafted sentences by the intelligent Magister were clear enough for the comfortably least mature being present to understand the main point. Although there was no Joxavian representative there present, it was clear that the Magister had been alluding to that particular species. The proclamation, however brutal it had come across, was clearly designed to restrain the powerful Joxavian army from immediately taking matters into their own hands and eliminating a substantial part of the human population. The human race might possess vast stockpiles of assorted weapons, including nuclear missiles, but they would still be powerless against such an advanced civilisation. It would not be a war, it would be an out and out massacre that would be over probably within a few hours.

"Thank you, sir. I think that I do understand. And I thank the committee and everyone else who wants to try and help. It sounds like our fate is in your hands, but I get the feeling that is a good thing."

"We are grateful to you for those kind words. I think we can now end this particular ordeal for you and allow you to spend some time that is less traumatic and hopefully both interesting and enjoyable. If you could please return the way you came to the waiting room, then someone will collect you from there and take you back to my office."

Alfred stood up and bowed his head in deference before turning around. He could see his scarlet-clad escort stood at the top of the stairs where he had entered the chamber, and was relieved to walk, a little shakily, to re-join him and exit the theatre. By comparison the waiting room now seemed a rather less unpleasant pleasant place to be.

# *Chapter Fourteen*

If there was one thing the earthling immediately needed it was a good hug. In lieu of his caring mother the next best thing was his caring tutor. As Alfred got back to the Magister's quarters he therefore had no hesitation in throwing his arms around the waiting Kriosta, who responded in kind, understanding the difficult and upsetting experience his ward had just undergone. Hopefully such occasions would be few and far between, although the future was now as uncertain as it had ever appeared. After fully a minute, with his composure reasonably restored, Alfred let go of his responsible adult and slumped down onto the middle of Grattin's comfortable lounge sofa.

"You know, sir, I am much too young to be allowed to drink alcohol, but from what I have seen in the movies, right now I think that I could do with a stiff drink, as they say."

Kriosta looked a little confused and did not respond, instead just sitting down next to the youngster. A few seconds later the door opened and the Magister came in. He looked a bit drained himself, and thankful to be back in his official home. Obviously old enough to pour himself a strong whiskey, it was clear that his preferred drink was Jesepian tea, so he headed for the dining table and a waiting pot of the brew. He emptied a portion into one of the large cups, then gratefully took a mouthful before offering some to his guests. Under normal conditions he would have tended to their needs first, however he appeared somewhat desperate; the others were more than happy to forgive the minor display of bad manners.

As Alfred sipped his offering, he briefly wondered whether anybody did actually drink alcohol on this planet, or indeed anywhere else in the universe. It was one of those strange questions that often just popped into his head as a consequence of being in such a totally peculiar environment. It was so different from his normal experience that it was unavoidable for his brain to keep generating a long list of queries and observations regarding the alien worlds and populations.

"Thank you for being so brave, Alfred. I thought you showed amazing courage for one so young, and so new to the task of having to interface with many new intelligent species."

"Well, to be honest, I surprised myself. I'm still trying to convince my stomach that I am brave though. I am just glad I got through it without being sick."

"Oh dear. Let me reassure you that the worst is over for the moment. In fact, I would like to invite you to a celebration dinner that we are having in your honour in the main refectory of the Grand Library this evening. You will get another chance to meet the council in less formal and daunting circumstances, as well as many of the staff and other students here who are really looking forward to talking to a genuine human being in this illustrious place of learning.

The guest of honour suddenly perked up. "That sounds nice. It sounds very nice. How kind."

"I think it is the least we can do considering what we just put you through." The Magister sat down on the right-hand side of the sofa. "Might I make a further suggestion? We would like to modify the itinerary that we had originally set out for you and insert a new item. Tonight, we would like you to sleep here, in a very nice nearby guest room that we have allocated to you. We also have a comfortable room for noble Kriosta, of course. Tomorrow, in a change to the advertised program, as you say on your planet, we would like to send you back to Earth for a little while."

"You mean go back home?"

"Actually, no." Grattin sipped his tea for several seconds, carefully working out his next words. "This is unfortunately another one of those brace yourself moments, although in this case what I am about to tell you is something that I am certain you will eventually be very pleased about, even if it completely shocks you to begin with."

"Here we go again," thought Alfred, managing to restrain himself from saying it out loud.

"Your species is by now quite familiar with the planet Mars, the next body out from your own in the solar system, having landing quite a few robotic exploration devices on its surface. As you know, there is no life on Mars. Well, the truth is, that is simply untrue."

"What?"

It was as well that Alfred was sitting on the Magister's sofa, sandwiched between the two big aliens, otherwise he might well have fallen off his chair. The head of the library waited for his astonishing pronouncement to begin to sink in before continuing.

There is no life visible on the surface of Mars, but there are a few, well, what you would call Martians, living underground. Only a few though, because, well, most of the rest of them are living on Earth."

Alfred froze into a sitting statue, making Grattin quite concerned about his physical, never mind mental, wellbeing.

"Master Alfred?" said Kriosta, placing a worried paw on the boy's left shoulder. Grattin placed a much more humanoid hand on his right shoulder. They both waited for some response that hopefully did not involve any visibly physical illness from their inexperienced young charge.

It took a good minute to finally gain an acknowledgement from the shaken earthling. "Alright. I think I am alright. Sorry about that. I don't know why I am so shocked. After all, I am quite used to the idea of aliens. I guess it is another thing to have them living alongside me on my own planet. But Martians. I mean, MARTIANS."

# *Chapter Fifteen*

The refectory was much larger than Alfred had expected, turning out to be not one room but instead six smaller rooms plus one enormous banqueting hall that could easily accommodate several hundred diners. It was quite full on this special evening, with about twenty tables catering for about twenty people each. The layout was decidedly egalitarian and cosmopolitan, with no obvious head table for the most senior attendees. That came as a relief to the little human guest of honour, who was enjoying the occasion and the friendly, quite informal atmosphere.

He was sitting once more sandwiched between Grattin and Kriosta, however the other guests at his table were all unfamiliar. There was a nice white tablecloth covering the surface, and three red candelabra features uniformly positioned along the length. The grey cutlery had a ceramic feel to it that matched the crockery upon which the food was being served, as well as the goblets for the more liquid refreshments. That trace of monotony was offset by some colourful napkins and a variety of glazed miniature ornaments and figurines dotted about.

The clientele were even more varied in both form and dress, to the point of dazzling the senses. It was a wonderful sight. About half of those present were either very humanoid or so close as to not to be obviously different. Of the remainder, there was still a predominance of one head, two eyes, two legs and two arms, however these individuals had a plethora of features that clearly distinguished them from the genus Homo sapiens. The most startling character, even more so than the octopus like creature Alfred had witnessed on the committee, was what could only be described as a bird. It had feathers anyway, and wings, and was wearing some strikingly chic clothes. The creature was located two tables away, chatting happily away to its fellow diners and enthusiastically raising a cup to its short, wide beak using a hand like appendage that rested at the ends of each of its two wings. It was such an extraordinary image that the astonished schoolboy had one of his not uncommon feelings that perhaps he was dreaming.

Just opposite from the earthling's own position, half way down the long side of a fairly central table, was the second youngest person in the room, going purely by subjective visual estimation. It may have been the case that this particular guest had deliberately been given that place setting as company for Alfred, to give him someone closer to his own age to talk to. If so it was a successful tactic, and the young earthling was keen to find out some more about him.

"Hello. Pleased to meet you. My name is Alfred."

His new acquaintance could not avoid giggling. "I think everyone here knows who you are, Alfred. My name is Sidereal. In case you were wondering, and you almost certainly were, I am twelve years old. If it makes you feel any better, I have just as much difficulty in trying to guess people's ages as you probably do."

Actually, it did make Alfred feel quite a lot better to learn this. Finally, here was somebody who also understood just how frustrating a thing it could be not to be able to tell how old other people were.

"Oh, thank so much for saying that. It has been driving me mad at times. That is a very nice name. Are you a student at the library?"

"Thank you, yes I am. My parents are both researchers here, so it was kind of a natural thing for me to study at the library's school for younger pupils. By the way, the school is the department you yourself are technically affiliated to. Basically, that makes us classmates!"

"My goodness. Well in that case I am doubly pleased to meet you, Sidereal. Your English is perfect. Where on Earth did you learn it? Oh dear, I must try to avoid using that expression. It really can be very inappropriate."

The alien youngster giggled again. "Don't worry, I understand. Strangely enough my parents did visit your planet for a few months and took me with them, so on this occasion your expression was valid since I did learn a lot of my English on Earth itself."

"Really? Amazing. How did they come to be there?"

Sidereal paused and thought before replying. "I can't say too much about that, but it was mainly as part of their research duties. It was not a long stay, but my race is very good at picking up languages, so I as was able to become fluent quite quickly. I also became a big fan of your movies and television programmes whilst I was there, which helped a lot."

Alfred shook his head in astonishment. "I'm sorry, but it is often so hard to take all the new things that I hear in. It is literally incredible at times."

A team of exclusively blonde waiters and waitresses, dressed in simple blue tunics identical to that of the steward Alfred had seen serving in Grattin's quarters, appeared from a side door that led to the kitchens. They were carrying large trays with various dishes of food placed onto them. Efficiently they began branching off to snake around the score of tables and deliver their tasty looking offerings. These young catering staff all looked slightly built, but it belied their obvious strength from the sheer quantity of foodstuffs that each of them was transporting.

One of them, an attractive young lady with very long hair that reached down to the back of her waist, arrived at Alfred's table, deftly unloading twelve large ceramic containers as she worked her way along the supporting structure. He could not help admiring her looks, her efficiency, and most of all her amazing physical power considering there was very little obvious muscle on her slender arms. The rules of nature frequently seemed difficult to follow in these far-off lands.

As she finished serving she politely curtseyed then headed off back towards the kitchens. Everyone then waited until the Magister reached over with his plate and helped himself to some of the available food dishes. As soon as he was finished the remaining diners, without further ceremony or delay, dived in and helped themselves too. Alfred, in a hard-core display of English politeness, waited till last before taking a share of the culinary spoils. There was more than enough to go around, so he was in no way disadvantaged by his manners. To his delight there was a generously filled basket of pink bread rolls, and they tasted just as good as he remembered them.

The remainder of the hour-long feast was completed quite casually, except for a short speech given by the Magister once more welcoming Alfred to the Grand Library. This drew an enthusiastic round of applause that prompted Alfred to stand up and nod in thanks to the four quarters of the assembled crowd in the refectory. It was incredibly nice of them all to give him such a reception, and he did appreciate it, but there was no getting rid of a feeling of embarrassment over the fact that he simply did not feel deserving of such recognition.

After this hoo-hah had subsided quite a few of the guests started to make their way out of the room and off to other activities, or perhaps their beds. By now Alfred was himself noticing a bit of fatigue setting in, which the intelligent Magister picked up on.

"It has been a long day for you, Alfred, but hopefully an interesting one. I will take you along to your guest room shortly where you can get some sleep, but first we would like to expand upon why we would like you to return to Earth tomorrow. Earlier I apprised you of the fact that there were Martians living clandestinely alongside your own race. There is one specific Martian that we now feel you should be introduced to without further delay. A very special lady. Actually, she is a Princess."

# *Chapter Sixteen*

"Are you sure this is the right address? I mean, it's not exactly a palace."

The house that they currently stood in front of was indeed hardly the sort of residence that one would expect a princess to be living in. This was no grand castle, but instead a very ordinary two storey terraced house, probably of Victorian vintage. Black slates covered a roof topped off with an old brick chimney, whilst black iron railings enclosed a small paved forecourt. There was a rectangular bay window on the right-hand side of the ground floor, to the left of which was an old green door sitting above a single whitewashed step. A brass knocker waited invitingly half way up the door, and above this sat a large well-polished brass number four.

"Yes, definitely right house. Number four. Like Mars. Fourth planet from sun."

Alfred wondered whether that was just a coincidence but did not pursue the matter. The evening was getting chilly and he was keen to get inside, also aware of the limited time slot they had for the visit. "In that case I shall knock the door."

The curtains were already closed even though dusk was technically still half an hour away. Alfred placed both feet upon the step and raised the knocker, hesitating for a moment before gingerly giving three gentle raps on the well glossed wood. He felt Kriosta's large frame huddling up just behind him.

Ten seconds passed without any response. The younger visitor was about to reach out his hand for another try when the latch clicked, and the door creaked open. To Alfred's surprise, it was not the Princess who initially received them but a tall, handsome young man with auburn hair and a visibly tanned face. He smiled before standing aside and beckoning the two arrivals into the dwelling. "Welcome. Please come inside."

Alfred froze momentarily at the sight of the young man, who looked human, but there was something about him that made the small visitor believe that standing before him was an actual Martian. Seriously. A genuine, real life Martian.

Kriosta noticed the near state of shock and smiled knowingly. He paused a few seconds before encouraging the earthling to enter with a very gentle push of his left paw between Alfred's shoulder blades. This had the desired effect as the still amazed boy traversed the white step and moved past his patiently waiting host, followed closely by his tutor, who put his right paw on the other alien's shoulder as he closed the door.

"Good see you again"

"Thank you, and so good to see you again. Please go straight through into the living room. The Princess will join you shortly."

"Thank you," said Alfred, standing aside to let the others lead the way as he did not know precisely where the living room was. It turned out to be the first door on the right. The hallway also led to a single door right at the end, and two equally spaced doors on the left. The hall carpet was light green. There was a single large framed photo of the red planet further down on the right-hand wall.

The lounge was a decent size, particular with respect to its length, and much bigger than that of Alfred's own home. It looked very traditional. There was a substantial three-piece suite covered in an attractive up market green and cream striped fabric, with the sofa pushed close to the wall opposite door. Midway along but on the other side adjacent to the door sat a beautiful marble hearth and fireplace surround, again in green and white, housing a realistic looking electric fire. A feature picture rail divided the lower and upper parts of the wall; the lower surface had a plain dark green wallpaper covering, whilst the upper area was painted in a clean, rich cream colour. The carpet was a luxuriously thick pile once more in cream. Further still down the room was a round teak wooden table with four matching chairs, a large sideboard fashioned from similar material against the right wall, and a tall bookcase in a darker wood that carried four shelves of densely packed books against the left wall. The extreme end of the room was largely covered by an extensive wall unit that contained a variety of electronic entertainment equipment, the centrepiece of which was a sixty-five-inch flat screen television that was currently switched off. At either side stood each of a pair of narrow floor standing loudspeakers with black cloth grilles.

"Can I get you some tea and biscuits?" asked the attendant whilst inviting the visitors to sit down on the sofa.

"Ooh, yes please. Milk but no sugar, thank you."

"Tea. Nice. Biscuits. Yes please. Milk and sugar for Kriosta. Thank you."

Their attentive host disappeared into what must have been the kitchen, leaving the guests sat waiting patiently, Alfred on the left with Kriosta to his right. As the seconds passed the young boy was starting to experience a familiar feeling of nervousness. It was quite something to be meeting a genuine princess, but the regal aspect was on this occasion completely overshadowed by the fact that the lady in question was a Martian. Having already come across several people whose origin was not from his own world he should by now perhaps be getting used to meeting such super foreigners. There was something different about this though, because the alien in question was from the nearest remotely habitable planet, a world that apart from being effectively a neighbour was also a world that had been the subject of endless cultural exploration and speculation. Great literary works by the likes of H. G. Wells, and Captain W. E. Johns, had considered the existence of a race native to the red planet, somewhat frighteningly in the case of the former author. Orson Welles had reputably managed to scare the wits out of those listening to his legendary radio broadcast when the residents of the United States had become convinced that they were actually being invaded by terrifying monsters from Mars. And now here he was, quietly and demurely awaiting the arrival of the real thing. What would those giants of the arts have made of this if they could have witnessed it for themselves?

There was some clinking of crockery audible from the kitchen, but other than this the room was hushed, adding greatly to the sense of occasion and anticipation. The level of tension was giving the poor boy extreme butterflies in his tummy, and he could have cut the atmosphere with a proverbial knife. It was the attendant who appeared first, carrying a packed tray of pots, cups, small jugs and biscuits, however as he approached the coffee table in front of the sofa the lounge door opened wide, and in strode a very beautiful golden-haired lady dressed in a predominantly light blue floral dress. Her flowing hair cascaded over the front of her shoulders, and as she clasped her hands in front of her waist a wide smile adorned her pretty face.

"Hello, Alfred, it is wonderful to meet you. And hello to you too Kriosta, it is marvellous to see you again. My name is Marlena. Welcome to my home."

The youngsters jaw dropped slightly in admiration. She seemed like some goldilocks of a woman, with everything looking just right.

"Thank you, your Royal Highness. This is a great honour for me." Somewhat belatedly he jumped to his feet as a mark of respect. Kriosta stood up also.

The lady looked to be in her late twenties, and there was absolutely nothing in her appearance to suggest her extraordinary genetic lineage, principally the fact that she was descended from an alien race.

"Why thank you. Ah, I'm glad to see that the tea has arrived. I don't know about you, but I am parched, and I could murder a custard cream."

The princess's relaxed demeanour put her small visitor more at ease, and he sat back down. Kriosta again copied his action. Her voice was clear and sweet, and despite the relatively common banter there was an unmistakeable upmarket elocution in the way that she spoke. She looked and sounded every bit the part of a royal princess. Alfred shuffled close to his tutor to make enough space for the lady to sit down. He realised that he had just become the filling in a most unusual sandwich.

"May I pour your tea for you, your Royal Highness?"

"Why thank you, and please, just call me Marlena. We do not stand on ceremony, normally."

"Thank you, I shall do that. Marlena. That's a lovely name; you don't hear it used very often these days. It suits you. Actually, thinking about it, I have just realised that it starts with MAR, as in Mars. I am guessing that is not just a coincidence."

"Well spotted. Yes, it was deliberate, although my parents and I really like the name anyway. I would be more than happy with it wherever I was from."

Kriosta took a sip from his cup, slurping slightly as he did so since his large jaws were not really designed for drinking from a small cup. He was about to devour a biscuit when he saw the other two simultaneously dunking their custard creams in their tea before consuming them, so he copied the action. The subsequent pleased look on his face indicated his approval of the technique. Unfortunately, his next biscuit disintegrated into the hot liquid as he left it submerged for too long, and Marlena could not help giggling at the dumfounded expression on Kriosta's face as he sat pinching the remaining one third, not quite comprehending what had just happened.

Alfred tried to console him but could not avoid laughing too. "Don't worry, sir. You will soon get the hang of it. Have another, but don't dunk it for so long."

Whilst his tutor tried again, this time successfully, the earthling took the opportunity to inquire further about his strange host. "I hope you don't mind me asking, but I am really curious about you and your people, and particularly the history of how you came to be here on Earth."

Marlena took on a more serious expression before replying. "Well, that is one reason for your visit today, so that you can learn a little about us. Hmm, where do I start? Well, I guess a good place would be to tell you about our civilisation as it used to be on our home planet of Mars, before we were forced by circumstances beyond our control to leave. Our race is much older than that of human beings. I mean many, many millions of years old. At that time Mars was very different to what it is now. Most importantly it had a much thicker atmosphere that could support life. It was also warmer, partly due to the atmosphere, but mainly because my race had evolved to the point where we had nuclear fusion reactors that were so powerful that they could augment the sun's rays sufficiently to keep the surface warm enough to sustain liquid water. Our civilisation was not large, about one million people covering the whole planet. Compare that to the current seven billion population of the human race, which has only really been around for tens of thousands of years, and only seven thousand years in any state that could be described as a formal civilisation.

"There was quite a bit of plant life, much of it cultivated by our farmers. There were no wars and no crime. I should hasten to point out that in the early days of our evolution we were naturally more primitive, and so was our behaviour, but by the time of the great catastrophe our society was both technologically and socially very advanced. Quite a utopia really. It was such a tragedy that it all came to an end one day, when we were ultimately forced to leave our home world. We have longed to go back and permanently live there again ever since."

Alfred had been so transfixed by the Princess's words that he had emulated his tutor's error by leaving a chocolate bourbon biscuit submerged beneath the surface of his cup of tea. As she paused her story he finally removed it, only to see it disintegrate and sink without trace. He quickly dunked what little was left before transferring it into his mouth. "That sounds really tragic," he said still chewing the biscuit, somewhat incongruously given the gravity of the topic. "May I ask what happened that was so serious that if obliged you to leave?"

Marlena hesitated before continuing, as though the subject was one that caused her great pain. "There was an enormous asteroid that came upon our planet with such speed that we had almost no notice of it. It was even bigger than the one that struck Earth about sixty million years ago and wiped out the dinosaurs. We were able to use our technology to divert it enough so that it did not directly hit Mars, but some large pieces broke off in the process and did strike the surface. Whilst most of the mass passed close by, the overall effect was to strip away much of the atmosphere and destroy nearly all the reactors and other machines. About ninety-nine percent of our race was wiped out, and our society was left completely devastated. Those that survived were forced to live a meagre subsistence below the surface of the red planet in underground structures that were not damaged in the catastrophe. They tried to rebuild as best they could, but it was hopeless. The survivors realised that the situation was beyond redemption, and a decision was made to use what few resources were left to create a vault, into which a large number of frozen embryos could be placed in the hope that one day they could be revived when circumstances allowed. It was quite simply survival mode for our species. The vault was sealed, with information about what had happened fixed to the door. Soon there were no people left alive as the food and oxygen ran out and the planet became very cold.

For millions of years it remained that way, an apparently lifeless world with all trace of our civilisation on the surface eroded into dust. If it were not for the intervention of another species from outside our solar system, my race would have become extinct. Fortunately, one day alien visitors arrived and found the vault. They were from a very advanced race who worked out what had happened and rescued the embryos, taking them back to their own home planet, where they were able to revive and nurture the remnants of the Martian population. We are, of course, eternally grateful for their caring actions. That had been our first exposure to people from other worlds. Thank goodness they turned out to be so intelligent and benign."

"I am so glad they came along to save you, and so sorry for what happened, and what your race went through. But there is one thing I do not understand. If they took the survivors to their world, how did some of you come to be living on the planet Earth?" Alfred, relieved at the relatively happy outcome considering the extreme tragedy that had befallen them, decided that it would not be a breach of etiquette to attempt another bourbon dunking, this time resolving to concentrate on that task as well as listening to his host.

"Well, that came about much, much later. The Martian race were made welcome on the new planet, which by the way we refer to as Olympus in your language, and there they stayed and evolved until about five thousand years ago. The Olympians travelled back to Mars and refurbished the subterranean buildings where the vault was located, so that we could have a base there that we could go and visit. One day it was hoped that the planet could be terraformed, allowing us to properly repopulate the surface. Later, when it was seen that a humanoid species, that is, Homo sapiens, had evolved to the point of developing its own civilisation, the people who administer the Galaxy decided that it would be acceptable to allow some Martians to come and live on Earth, since it was the nearest habitable planet to Mars itself. They ferried us here and inserted us into a small colony at a particular location. Our settlers brought along some advanced technology to help them, with the proviso that it was not to be revealed to the indigenous population. They adhered to that, although it was impossible to avoid at least some exposure to some of your ancient tribes, such as the Egyptians."

Alfred chuckled gently. "My goodness. That does seem to explain some of the ancient alien conspiracies that have arisen over the years, particularly from certain early drawings."

"Indeed. It is amusing in a way, although there has also been concern about the number of genuine sightings of visiting craft there have been. It is getting increasingly difficult to hide the truth."

There was a natural pause in the discussion whilst everyone sipped their tea. Eventually, Alfred shook his head slowly before stating the obvious. "What a truly wonderous story."

"Yes, amazing," agreed Kriosta. "So good Martian people saved. Very good people."

"Thank you." The Princess sat back and folded her arms, then turned her head to stare directly down at her young visitor. "We are not from your planet, and however grateful we are for being able to reside here, we yearn to be able to leave in the future and go back to live on Mars. But during the time we have been here we have developed a great affection for the Earth. There is such natural beauty here that many species have described it as the jewel of our galaxy. Which makes it all the more difficult for me to have to say the following. Many species, on many other worlds, have sat and watched with dismay the development of humanity from a small population whose global impact was relatively minor, to a vast population that has become by far the dominant species on Earth, and whose impact is no longer minor but now overriding. This is personally heart-breaking for myself as I love nature, and the fabulous variety of plants and animals that you have here. I know that many humans share my concerns, and I am sure that you do too."

Alfred was embarrassed by the lady's unexpectedly frank statement. He knew her words were justified, and as the only human in the room their force was focused hard on his own small, young frame. This felt like his appearance before the Galactic committee all over again. He was sure that the intention had not been to cause him distress, but he gulped hard and his face became visibly flushed. It was not physically easy to reply, and in any case what words could he have said in response to such a charge.

The Princess took hold of Alfred's left hand with her right. "There are a lot of good humans, definitely including you, young man. I thought it best to be very upfront about the matter; rest assured that we are here to help where we can."

The humbled earthling felt better for the kind compliment and friendly support. He managed to smile a little, then finally reply, "Thank you, your highness. I get the impression that we are lucky to have your people here."

Marlena leant forward to be able to speak directly to Kriosta, and her expression changed markedly to something much more cheerful. "Do you think you could take us for a little ride to somewhere warmer for a short visit? I love England, and my home here, but the weather can be somewhat grim. I think it might be better if we continued getting to know each other with a bit of sun on our backs."

"Good idea. Go Arizona."

"What a good suggestion. I will just go and get my things. I'll be ready in five minutes. I suggest that you freshen up, my attendants will look after you."

"What? Excuse me? Arizona? Do you mean, as in America?"

"Yes. The Grand Canyon to be exact. One of my favourite places for a picnic."

Considering he had just travelled halfway across the galaxy, the idea of nipping over to the United States of America as if they were getting a taxi down to the local shops should really have been no big thing. Unfortunately, his young human psyche was still nowhere near being used to it yet. He did not expect to become used to it any time soon, either.

# *Chapter Seventeen*

"Oh my goodness. Magnificent."

"Yes. Much beautiful."

"Words fail me, sir."

"Gentlemen, I have to agree with you. What an amazing planet this is."

The Princess was perched leaning with her torso in-between Alfred and Kriosta as the pair sat in the pilot and co-pilot's seats of the furriest alien's spaceship. It had come gently to rest atop one of the cliff faces that made up the vast panorama of the Grand Canyon in the state of Arizona in the United States of America.

"We land North Rim of canyon," explained Kriosta. "Closed to public this time of year. More private."

"Good thinking," commented Alfred. The spaceship was currently invisible to outside observers, however it was additionally good practice to avoid being around human beings if convenient. Perhaps a brief glimpse of its not so sleek lines might make the lives of the local UFO conspiracy theorists a bit more interesting, but if one of them managed to snap too good a photo, something clearer than the traditional very blurry snap you often saw on the television, then that would be worse than merely embarrassing for the off-world visitor.

It was early afternoon and the sun was near its peak overhead. The plan was to get out and stroll around to do a bit of sightseeing. It would be warm and pleasant outside, although this journey was not completely just about sightseeing. The Princess had arranged the trip so that they could continue to get to know each other better. That was no bad thing as Alfred had already developed a great liking for the beautiful and charming lady.

Kriosta eased his way out of the pilot's seat and led the trio to the main entrance door, unlocking it using a small lever before pushing it wide open. The air outside swept in aided by a warm breeze, ruffling the hairs of the fur on the alien's head. He climbed down onto the stone surface before turning to lift the small earth boy out to join him, and then lending a right paw to Malena to assist her own egress. Kriosta closed the door as the three shook off the cramp from their constricted journey. He then walked a few paces away towards the edge of the nearby steep drop to the canyon below, halting at a suitably safe distance to avert any danger of falling over. They stood and admired the wide vista of the American national park for a minute without speaking, entranced by the sight. Kriosta then wandered away a few metres to leave the other two more alone.

Alfred watched him go before turning to face the Princess, who took on a grim expression.

"I suggested we come here for another reason than just to do some sightseeing Alfred. I very much had an ulterior motive. There is something important that I must tell you, and this place, one of the finest locations on this beautiful planet, seemed to be an appropriate place to do it."

Alfred looked perplexed at the announcement. It had not occurred to him that the trip might be anything other than a tourist visit, with a little bit of a bonding exercise thrown in for good measure. "That sounds a little worrying".

Marlena's facial expression did not change from a quite stern and serious look, which hardly reassured the young earthling. So far, she had been nothing but a paragon of sweetness and charm. "There is nothing to be alarmed about at the moment, but I want to be completely honest with you, so I must admit that there is some cause for you and everyone else on earth to be concerned. Let me speak frankly."

The Princess sat down on a nearby flat slab of rock, folding her arms before beckoning Alfred over with her a flick of her head, the medium length trestles of her hair floating in the soft wind as she did so. He complied with the request but remained standing as she continued.

"There are many interesting worlds throughout the galaxy, and yes, many other beautiful planets. However, the Earth is beyond compare when it comes to the diversity of its geography, flora and particularly fauna, or plants and wildlife if you like. Nowhere else quite matches it for all round magnificence. But therein lies the problem. The extraordinary richness of the natural world is being threatened by a species that is so utterly dominant that it has for some time now been interfering with everything else on the surface and beneath the seas to the point where the sheer destruction of the environment and other creatures poses a catastrophic risk to their future. Already countless species have become extinct solely because of the effects of the massive expansion of the human race over the last thousand years."

The emotional immaturity of the ten-year-old did not mean that he was short of emotions, and the two that came to the fore now were embarrassment and shame. The unexpectedness of what was coming across as a dressing down, even though he was sure that had not been the Princess's intention, was making it hard for him to maintain his composure. The Martian lady sensed this and gestured to him to sit down beside her to make it look less like a teacher scolding a pupil.

"Please sit down beside me, Alfred. I know that there are many good humans, indeed many who are themselves trying to help stop the bad things that have been happening, and their goodness has been recognised and appreciated by other races throughout the galaxy. And I certainly count you as one of those good humans." Alfred complied and took his place on the rock close by her right-hand side, feeling a tiny bit better. "It is a very difficult situation, and not at all easy for myself and the other descendants of the original population of Mars. We are somewhat caught in the middle because we have lived on this planet for so long that we can undoubtedly be considered as naturalised citizens of the planet Earth, and yet we definitely consider ourselves as primarily still Martians. As I said at the house, our hope is that one day we can return to live permanently on our own world. Given our special status, it also places upon us a special responsibility to contribute to saving the natural world. However, there is not much that we can do directly, although we do put in much indirect effort to helping those humans who are willing and able to make a difference. Above all else it makes my people very sad to see what is going on, and I have spent many days in my long life, particularly in the last hundred years, sitting and crying at what I see happening."

The princess had temporarily lost her aura of aloof royalty and seemed close to tears now. It was clear that her love of the natural world was paramount, and that she genuinely felt tortured by what the human race as a whole were doing. Alfred felt so sorry for her, and he gently clasped both his hands around her right hand as she dropped it onto the blue cotton dress that covered her knees.

The sun had stubbornly held its place high above and its bright powerful rays kept the temperature high enough to help ward off some of the depression that had clouded the mood of the visitors. The boy from cool rainy England squinted in the brightness, maintaining enough of an aperture between his eyelids to gaze out over the beautiful scenery as the pair fell silent for a contemplative moment. Nearby a couple of large birds that he took to be condors were circling the air adjacent to the cliff edge, their enormous wings spread out in an effortless glide through the rising updraft of a strong thermal. This paradise just emphasised the alien lady's sadness at the ongoing destruction of the environment in less protected locations around the world.

A pair of tears trickled down the perfect complexion of Marlena's cheeks. Alfred did not know how to react, but fortunately the older and wiser Kriosta, who had been keeping his distance whilst monitoring the conversation with his ultra-keen hearing, came calmly over to help out. Without speaking he sat by the Princess's left side and reached round to put a big comforting paw on her right shoulder. She tilted her head to rest it on his caring frame, managing a half-smile through the tears. And there the three sat quietly in the wonderful warmth for the next five minutes, enjoying the magnificent planet as it should be.

It was the noise of an unmistakably terrestrial flying machine that roused them from their short spell of meditation as a small single piston-engined aeroplane began to approach from the direction of the opposite side of the canyon. There was no reason to believe that it was specifically coming to take a look at the trio, nevertheless it could potentially be an issue if it came close enough for the occupants to get a good luck at the furriest of the unusual tourists. At a distance they might mistake him for a grizzly bear, yet the smoking jacket plus proximity to the other two would surely warrant a more thorough investigation.

The two aliens glanced nervously at each other, and then both stared over to the approaching object of their concern. There was no cover to hide under here, just bare rock with a liberal smattering of dust along with a threadbare covering of small shrubs. It was probably already too late to head for the shelter of the spaceship; that might look even worse if caught on camera when the scurrying hulk of Kriosta suddenly vanished from view apparently into thin air.

As luck would have it the Princess did have one trick up her sleeve, or rather in the medium sized shoulder bag that she had brought with her and which was presently lying at her feet where she had put it down whilst they talked. From it she pulled a wide brimmed folded up floppy hat that she hastily unfurled and pressed onto the blatantly alien head of her friend. It was very large, very floppy, and had a rather feminine floral lavender pattern, but it did the trick. Kriosta looked suitably ridiculous, distinctly awkward, and extremely funny in this unexpected attire. Alfred could not help laughing at the sight, however serious the purpose, and the Princess was clearly trying her best not to snigger also. It was a necessary ruse, and often the first casualty of necessity is dignity. The expression on the alien's face was impossible to see since it was hidden by the collapsed edges of the soft fabric headgear, but maybe that was just as well.

The plane came nearer, before banking to one side and heading off down the valley following the course of the Colorado River. Alfred and the Princess gave an innocent wave to the aircraft as it departed innocuously. Resisting the temptation to whip out his mobile phone to take a mischievous photograph, Alfred removed the hat and handed it back to the Martian lady, who finally burst out laughing uncontrollably at the sight of Kriosta's stony look of not quite knowing what was going on.

When they were confident that they were completely isolated again, it was his tutor who unexpectedly returned to the topic that had so distressed the Princess.

"Many worried about Earth. As Princess say. But big problem one race from Galaxy edge. Called Joxavians. Not like others. More fierce. Sometimes frighten others. Powerful weapons. Very scary race."

Alfred became immediately worried by this confirmation of what he had already been told. "Yes, I am becoming all too familiar with those alien gentlemen." He looked over at Marlena for further clarification."

"I'm afraid it's true. They are not normally aggressive and do not as a rule go around causing trouble, but they have very firm views about things in general, and Earth in particular; they are indeed prepared to use force when they think it is needed. And they are particularly unhappy with the human race. The galactic council have so far managed to keep them from taking any action, but that gets more difficult with each passing year. Honestly, it is getting to the point where they cannot be constrained for very much longer. There is much discussion at the council as to what they can do to solve this problem. Which is one reason that we are having this conversation. They would like you to go and meet with representatives of the Joxavian race on their home planet."

"Me? But what on earth can I do to help? I am nobody. I'm just an ordinary young boy."

"You are certainly not a nobody, although I agree you have no formal position of authority, or much experience. In this case though, that is an advantage. They do not want some duplicitous, self-serving politician trying to speak for the whole of your species, they just want to speak to a normal person. There is nothing to worry about as regards meeting the Joxavians, even if they are a little intimidating to meet at first because of their reputation. I have to warn you though that whilst your safety is assured, I won't lie about the fact that such a trip will be no picnic. I absolutely reiterate though that you will not personally be in any danger."

The wonderful location and warm sunshine were now struggling to keep Alfred's spirits up as the message about what lay ahead for him began to sink in. It was bad enough that the Earth appeared to be in trouble with the dangerous Joxavians, but the thought that he would be asked to visit their planet was disturbing. For the first time since his exposure to the terrifying hypercats he was beginning to wonder if it might have been better if he had not stumbled upon the Galactic Wide Web.

# *Chapter Eighteen*

During the remainder of their all too short journey to North America the Princess had given Alfred a concise briefing about the history of her race from the Red Planet. How many years, how many thousands of centuries had passed while the descendants of the original Martian population had been in their state of preservation was not certain. The only remaining physical traces of the old civilisation were buried beneath the surface of the modern-day planet. They had never been fully excavated by the handful of non-indigenous visitors that had since landed on the now barren world. The reconstruction work that had enabled the current Martian population to at least have a foothold back on their home world had been done five thousand years ago, long before the advent of telescopes on Earth that might have revealed the operation to prying human eyes. That had been ten thousand years after the discovery of the frozen embryos and their removal to Olympus where the process of restoration had been completed.

The decision to integrate the Martians into the fledgling civilisations of Europe and North Africa was taken around the time of the building of the first pyramids in ancient Egypt, beginning with a small colony of less than fifty. Their arrival on Earth had been very discrete, aided by the presence of several specialists from the Grand Library who were schooled in the culture and language of that remarkable age of human development. The colony had been based in Alexandria on the north coast of Egypt, where it remained for several hundred years before trebling in size and establishing outposts in Rome and Athens.

The refugees from the red planet had an extremely long lifespan compared to humans. This meant that it was practically impossible to mix with Homo sapiens in any biological sense, even if that had been allowed. So, the Martians had largely kept themselves to themselves throughout the years. They had regularly left for visits to Mars, and to spend prolonged periods on Olympus too. In order to make such trips it had been necessary to bring in transportation in the form of flying saucers, which had inevitably led to occasional sightings over the three millennia up to the twenty-first century.

Alfred found it a little amusing to realise that flying saucers really had existed and visited the earth after all, and that the many reports of their presence by countless people considered to be cranks and publicity seekers were in fact in many instances true. Actually, there had not been that many genuine sightings, but he did feel sorry for those unfortunate observers who had not been taken seriously when reporting their close encounters to the authorities.

The young fan of all things space had always been interested in watching documentaries on television about sightings of UFO's, and like many such enthusiasts he was very keen to know the truth about the infamous Roswell incident, way back in the nineteen-forties. This was where an alien spacecraft had allegedly crash landed in the southern part of the United States, and alien bodies had reputedly been recovered from the crash site by the Government. It was also close by to a place known as Area 51, an Airforce base where secret research was conducted into a variety of new flying machines.

His opportunity to become acquainted with real life aliens seemed a natural and perfect opportunity to finally find out what had really transpired at Roswell. It was therefore with the greatest chagrin that he had received an unwelcome reply that neither Marlena nor Kriosta were allowed to comment upon the matter. "Oh no, you're kidding me," had been his slightly too frustrated response to the polite but firm refusal. Both aliens were adamant though, and he had no choice but to accept their official position and hope that it would not be too long before he was allowed to know.

After that disappointing let down, his mood was reconstituted by an extraordinary invitation by the Princess. The trio had just taken off to head back to England, and Alfred was sitting in the main cabin keeping Marlena company whilst Kriosta sat alone in the cockpit performing his pilot's duties.

"Alfred, I am so pleased that you have lived up to the very high opinion of you that Kriosta clearly held when he first mentioned to me that you had stumbled upon the Galactic Wide Web, with all that implied. I must tell you that I was initially quite alarmed at that news, but now I am really glad that it happened. You are a credit to the human race."

Alfred was taken aback at the unexpected praise, and just replied with a simple, "Thank you, your Highness." He knew just what praise it truly was, coming from the leader of the Martian population.

"As a reward for you being so wonderful I would like, on behalf of my people, to formally invite you to come and visit us on our own planet. Our base there is small, but I cannot tell you how important it is to us. Having a home there, however humble, means everything. I love the Earth, but as you are fond of saying here, there's no place like home."

"I understand. I feel exactly the same about where I live. It is only a small house, but I would not swap it for a mansion. Gosh, I don't know what to say. That is so kind of you. Wow, a trip to Mars. I mean, words fail me. Actually, that seems to be happening a lot these days."

Alfred shook his head, once more finding it all a bit difficult to deal with. The Princess reached over and gave his hand a quick comforting squeeze. "There's nothing to worry about. I think that you will really enjoy the experience. Our base is small yet very comfortable. It was built by the marvellous people from Olympus, who rescued us from oblivion after our extremely long period of hibernation following the great disaster that befell our planet. They are the most advanced race in the galaxy, and to be honest a bit mysterious in their ways. They very much value their privacy, so even I do not know that much about them. One thing is beyond doubt though, they are both wise and good, and you would not be talking to yours truly if it were not for their intellect and generosity."

"Well then, they have my everlasting gratitude."

It did not take long before the coastline of west Wales announced that they were back in the green and pleasant land of the United Kingdom. They would be dropping Marlena off first before remaining out of time and rocketing back out into the galaxy.

"One question that I have about the trip to Mars. How do we get there? Will Kriosta be taking us?"

"Good heavens, no. There are quite a few of us scheduled to go there soon, so we will be taking the bus."

"The what? The bus? The BUS?"

# *Chapter Nineteen*

Following his introduction to the wonderful Princess, it was time to return to the Grand Library. The quaint little guest bedroom that they had assigned to him was basic yet still a nice place to be. There was no television or radio, and it was extremely quiet, to the point that he suspected there must be some hidden technology working behind the scenes to facilitate this peaceful condition. Not that the library was an inherently noisy place anyway, quite the reverse; it was a hallowed seat of learning, with a pervading atmosphere of intellect and respect amongst those working and studying within its buildings and grounds. His various activities since leaving his beloved Mother behind on Earth had been fairly intense and emotionally draining, meaning that he was more than content just to be able to lie in the comfortable bed that evening and catch up on some badly needed shuteye.

In the morning he rose at eight o'clock, according to his watch. It was still running on Earth time, as strictly speaking he also was, but by a happy coincidence this did not seem to be far removed from the local time. He had been told that this planet was forty percent larger than his own, however it rotated at a similar angular rate, leaving the length of day at a little over twenty-three hours. Midnight was a few minutes ahead of Greenwich Mean Time, certainly close enough to forego any risk of jetlag, or in this case spaceship lag.

After performing a short set of ablutions, he opened the door to his tiny temporary pad and walked down the corridor to a flight of steps that led down to the refectory. The main hall was far less busy than during the recent feast held in his honour. There was nobody there that he particularly recognised, so he looked around awkwardly wondering what to do. One of the blue tunic clad catering staff noticed him and helpfully directed him to a table in one of the smaller rooms overlooking the rear of the building. She informed him that he could order whatever he wanted to since they were able to provide anything from a typical breakfast menu that he was used to at home.

He decided to treat himself to some porridge with a few blueberries, some wholemeal bread toast and marmalade, and a pot of English Breakfast Tea. The young lady marched off to prepare his meal, leaving Alfred to gaze out of the window wondering what this fresh day would bring. The answer was not long in coming as Grattin appeared in the doorway leading out to the main hall. Having located his guest, he came over to chat once more with the young boy from Earth.

"Good morning. I hope you slept well."

"Very well, sir."

"Excellent. We thought it might be an idea to give you a relatively stress-free day today, you will be pleased to hear. We have something lined up that we think you will find quite fascinating, and hopefully quite good fun too in its own way."

"Actually, that sounds good. I could use a more relaxing day. That does not mean that I regret coming, and I am most grateful for everyone's fantastic hospitality. It has not been easy on the nerves at times though."

"I fully understand. We do appreciate your courage and forbearance. I'll let you enjoy your breakfast first, but afterwards if you could pop up to my office then I will fill you in on the details. You will have to take a train to another location on this planet, however that will at least give you chance to get a picture of the rest of the city, and also some of the country side in this region. Anyway, take your time, there's no hurry."

The Magister departed. It did not take long for the food and drink to arrive, and not unexpectedly it turned out to be unashamedly delicious. Whatever else the alien civilisations were good or bad at, they all certainly seemed to have mastered the art of cordon bleu cooking. Not as good as his mother's, of course, but still superb.

His ever-curious mind had been working overtime during breakfast trying to second guess what the course administrators had organised for him to do today. Nothing could have prepared him for what Grattin eventually revealed.

"Are you telling me that I am going to be travelling back in time?"

"Not exactly. Yes and no, basically."

"What did you call this place that I will be visiting today?"

"The Time Telescope. It is a device that we developed relatively recently; it became fully operational only thirty years ago. The equipment is based in the Historical Ministry, whose current location was chosen specifically to allow enough room to house the giant telescope, hence the need to take a train to reach the area. Strictly speaking, it allows us to look back in time rather than travel in time, but its sophistication is such that it gives people the opportunity to experience in great detail what it was like to live in past ages. Needless to say, the telescope provides us with an extremely accurate research tool."

Anything to do with time, from a physics point of view, was of utmost interest to Alfred. He was aware of the ability to control the flow time that existed amongst some civilisations, but this seemed to be something entirely different.

# *Chapter Twenty*

The journey time to the Historical Ministry was only fifteen minutes, and was spent mostly in silence, despite being accompanied by his new friend Sidereal. Alfred continued to be quite tired so was aware of the need to try and pace himself more steadily, if possible. He was also fascinated by the scene outside the window as they travelled along a raised railway, which afforded an excellent uninterrupted view of the surrounding countryside and occasional buildings.

The terrain was a strange mix of desert, grassland, lakes and forest, actually a bit of everything except hills or indeed any significant elevation.

As for the buildings, well they were sparse and irregularly distributed, however each seemed to be magnificently designed and beautifully constructed to the highest standards. The majority seemed to be residential dwellings the size of a large five-bedroom detached house back on earth, occupying a generous plot of about an acre. The architecture was very unbritish though, more Mediterranean; some looked like roman villas, some more Moroccan with whitewashed walls. One particularly ostentatious structure resembled a small palace from ancient times with a multitude of large marble like columns. They nearly all had very pretty gardens, displaying flowers of every conceivable colour.

There were a few obviously different very plain buildings with little or no gardens that did not look like homes but whose function was not immediately obvious. None of them were very high. That made it all the more spectacular when Alfred finally caught sight of their destination as the railway veered off in a slow sweep to the right.

Kriosta had mentioned that the Time Telescope was housed in a very tall building, although that turned out to be the most major of understatements. This was far more than merely tall, the thick central cylindrical tower seemed to rise without end, reaching up into the sky beyond the limit of Alfred's vision. He could only sit in complete awe and astonishment as they moved rapidly closer. It became obvious that the building at the bottom of the tower was itself very extensive, a square base that had sides each approaching a kilometre in length. The height was perhaps ten stories, although this was difficult to judge as there were no windows in the outer walls, save for what might be several apertures in a small part of the ground floor half way along the right-hand side. It was still too far away to tell for sure, but that must be where the entrance to the building was located.

The speed of the train was faster than anything Alfred had experienced on Earth, although he had not actually spent that much time on the terrestrial network. Regrettably, the English railway system was not the best, and certainly not the quickest on his own planet. For a country that had invented the railways, back in the small town of Shildon in the North-East of England, it was rather depressing to see the state of British public transport in the twenty-first century. At least some countries were more ambitious and advanced, notably the bullet train in Japan, and the proposed Hyperloop system in the United States that promised speeds competitive with those of airliners.

The train in which he currently sped towards their destination was extremely comfortable, very quiet, and very spacious. Sidreal had been very amused at the idea of separate classes when Alfred had asked about this at the station. There was only one class for everyone on this extremely civilised world, but this standard class was luxurious to the point where Alfred could have happily stayed cruising in his plush seat for hours on end.

That was not going to happen on this occasion, as the three carriages drew swiftly nearer to the enormous structure ahead; after only another minute the train began to decelerate as it reached the nearest corner. The raised line had gradually descended to the level of the ground floor. Soon it was obvious that what he had suspected to be the entrance was just that, and he could now confirm that there were some large windows surrounding a smallish porch housing a glass door. There was a long platform located just outside the entrance, comfortably longer than the three carriages. The train came to a stop conveniently in the middle of this.

"Welcome to the legendary Time Telescope, Alfred," announced Sidreal, finally breaking the self-imposed silence.

"Thank you. I can hardly believe it. The building is huge, but that tower in the middle, that is something else."

"Impressive, isn't it?"

"Do you know how high it actually is?"

"Well, that is not as simple a question as you might think. We can revisit that question in the future. For now, shall we alight and go inside?"

"Oh, er, yes, of course. Don't want to keep the driver waiting."

"The driver?"

"Oops, sorry, I forgot that it is all automatic."

The few other passengers onboard had left their seats and moved to the doors at either end of the carriage. Alfred hurriedly rose and followed them, nervous about missing the stop. There were a small number of people waiting to get on for the return journey, and they patiently waited for everyone to get off before boarding themselves. All of the other alightees walked down the platform heading for a sunken door some fifty metres away. Sidereal instead guided his new acquaintance across a short gangway that led to the main entrance, a double glass panelled door whose halves automatically slid open to grant the newcomers access. As the duo entered they could hear the train just starting to move off again with its fresh cargo.

The first impression that Alfred had of the interior of the building housing the Time Telescope was that it was not at all what he had been expecting. Rather than rows of offices, or banks of super advanced machines and computers, the enormous entrance hall had almost no technical equipment. Instead, it looked like a giant arboretum with trees large and small, along with bushes and colourful flowers surrounding a large central pond. Cascading into this was a miniature waterfall, actually not that miniature, which draped a rocky outcrop situated on the far side from the entrance. In truth the only non-natural accoutrement in the hall was what appeared to be a reception area built into the right-hand side, where a solitary white-bearded old man dressed in a white robe with a purple apron stood waiting patiently and silently. He was dwarfed by the rest of the tranquil scene. Bright yellow artificial light descended from the far-left corner of the internal space as if from a sun powering through a hole in the clouds of a dull afternoon.

Alfred marvelled at the sight briefly, before Sidereal put his right hand behind the boys back and pointed towards the reception desk. "I think we need to check in over there," he spoke quietly.

The pair began to walk in that direction along a tiled yellow path that skirted the nearest edge of the pond, the route looking like it might have been plundered from the set of 'The Wizard of Oz'. Alfred half expected a youthful Frances Gumm to suddenly appear from nowhere and start skipping along it.

The Methuselah like man waiting to welcome the visitors at the reception counter greeted them in a clear, powerful voice that would have not been out of place on the stage of the Royal Shakespeare Company. "My name is Higonius. This is the Historical Ministry, which contains the great Time Telescope. Beyond here lies all that has been, and all that has led to your existence. Understand this, all who now pass."

A shiver ran up the earthling's back at the profound words that perfectly put into context where he was and what he was about to do.

"Who stands before Higonius?"

"My name is Alfred, from the planet Earth."

"And I am Sidereal, from the planet Sidigus".

"All who wish to enter must sign the Roll of Time."

The strict receptionist gestured towards a huge open book laid atop the counter, which was a little high for the short legs of the ten-year-old so that he had to stand up on his tiptoes to get a clearer view of its contents. The pages were of an expensive looking velum like material and ruled closely with three columns.

"You have to enter your name, species and place of origin," whispered Sidereal helpfully. Alfred complied using an enormous wooden pen plucked from its vertical stand just to the right of the thick document, writing Alfred Smith, human, and planet Earth. He then eased himself down onto his flat feet and stood aside to allow his alien classmate to follow suit.

It felt like quite an honour to have his name writ large, or actually not so large considering the compact space available, in the important sounding Roll of Time. After they had both completed the obligatory task Higonius bowed his head. "Please follow me," he announced, before turning to walk through a heavily carved golden archway.

The opening led into a short tunnel, on the other side of which was a spacious lounge that appeared to be some sort of waiting area. Sidereal confirmed this, having already had the benefit of prior excursions to the Historical Ministry. The receptionist instructed them to take a seat, and then departed through a green door at the far end of the room.

There was nobody else present. The others who had travelled with them on the train had clearly been workers at the Ministry since they had headed straight for what appeared to be the tradesmen's entrance. How many employees there were could have been anything given the staggering size of the building.

"I must say that I am very nervous," confessed Alfred. The pair were sitting facing each other ensconced in comfortably cushioned single chairs.

"Understandable. I was too on the first occasion that I came here. In fairness, it is a daunting thing, however the staff here know that and are extremely friendly. I know Higonius seems very formal, perhaps even intimidating in his manner, but he has a heart of gold. Bear in mind also that it is a very important and honourable position that is only given to people of great age and standing within the galactic community. I know that before this he worked as a researcher for many centuries at the Library."

"I see."

It was several minutes before the receptionist reappeared, pausing just inside the far door. A second later someone else entered. It was another elderly looking gentleman, this one, however, more late middle age than very old. He was clean shaven with closely cropped grey hair, and in stark contrast to his colleague was dressed in completely black robes.

This is the Timekeeper, Master Alfred. He will accompany you from here."

"Thank you. Pleased to meet you, sir"

"Please, come through," requested the newcomer in a sombre voice. "Sidereal, would you please remain in the waiting area for the moment."

Alfred rose from his seat and gave a salutary wave to his new friend as he followed the Timekeeper out through the green door. The barrier opened automatically to allow them into a metallic walled corridor that ran for some twenty metres to a second green door. This again opened by itself and led into an elevator car, also with grey metallic walls. It was only large enough to hold four people at a time.

When the ensuing short vertical journey ended, the lift door slid open to reveal yet another corridor, this one rather wider and much, much longer, indeed so long that it was a strain to see what lay at the far end of it.

There were doors placed every fifty metres or so along both sides, arranged so that the left-hand doors were midway between the right-hand doors. The walls were again grey metallic, but the route was more brightly lit than had been the case before. How many doors there were was impossible to even guess since the corridor might well have run the entire length of the huge building.

"We are going to the fourteenth door on the left, Master Alfred."

The visitor's heart sank a little since that looked quite a distance for his small legs to walk. Just as he was resigned to starting the long trek he noticed something very unusual away in the distance, a sort of bright shimmering glare that seemed to be getting closer. It did not remain in the distance for very long as it quickly became evident that whatever it was the object was hurtling nearer at considerable speed, so quickly that Alfred began to get worried that it was going to ram right into them. In less than a trice it was close enough for him to make out what it was. The object was a silvery thin metal sheet, marginally narrower than the width of the corridor and floating at a height of not much more than an inch above the floor. He gasped as it approached with no sign of slowing, but then was relieved to see it suddenly decelerate to a crawl and then stop just in front of the pair.

The Timekeeper, who was obviously expecting this virtual missile, looked completely unfazed, unlike his shaken up young guest. "May I ask what this is?" inquired Alfred, trying his best to sound composed and calm, despite being neither.

"It is a transport mat. It will quickly take us to our destination without having to walk there. Time for you is very precious."

"A transport mat? You mean it's a sort of high tech flying carpet?"

The Timekeeper took on a puzzled expression before smiling as he recalled what the colloquial phrase meant. "Ah yes, I see, from your ancient fables. I suppose you could call it that. Rather amusing."

With that the alien took a tiny step up onto the flimsy looking but actually completely rigid sheet, shuffling to take a position just right of the centre. He then twisted round patiently waiting for his visitor to join him. Alfred tentatively obliged, positioning himself just to the left of centre. After a few seconds he felt the mat gently moving off, thankfully remaining at a much more modest speed than it had achieved during its original approach.

The ride was exceptionally stable and smooth, making the ever-curious earthling wonder what mechanism allowed the mat to glide so effortlessly along, and what material it was made of.

"The mat is made of a very stiff room temperature superconductor," announced the timekeeper unexpectedly. "There is a reversible phased magnetic field built into the floor that forces the mat to move in the desired direction.

"Can you read my mind, sir?" replied Alfred, somewhat startled at having his thought questions answered.

"No, but I could sense your curiosity, and I have been told that you are intelligent and have a very inquiring mind."

"Thank you. I have to say that my brain can barely contend with everything that I am coming across. I do appreciate the amazing experiences that I am being treated to, but it really is enough to freak out Albert Einstein, never mind little me. I mean, I am happy to admit that I'm really nothing special."

"Well, maybe not on paper. You ended up here by accident, however from talking to various people the consensus is that you are very highly thought of. Perhaps it was not so accidental. The universe is a very strange place. If you think we understand it completely just because we are so technologically advanced, then you could not be more wrong. As one of your own great scientists once famously put it, 'Anyone who is not shocked by quantum theory has not understood it.'"

"That was Niels Bohr who said that, I believe."

"Well there you are, young man; how many ten-year-old boys from the planet Earth have heard of that quote and know who said it? You should definitely not underestimate yourself."

"Well, thank you once more, but I certainly feel quite ordinary. Anyway, I am at least extremely grateful for the privilege of being here."

"Well said."

The intervening right and left-hand doors did not exactly flash past, but it was still much quicker and easier than walking, and Alfred was appreciative of having been able to hitch a ride on the simple yet remarkably effective transport mat.

The fourteenth door on the left duly became the next one, causing the mat to ease to a halt a yard short of it. Alfred followed the timekeeper off the silver plate, then briefly looked back towards the lift. He was surprised at just how far off it now looked and realized that they had been moving deceptively quickly.

"Would you care to enter?"

The door clicked and swung ajar. Alfred cautiously pushed it far enough open to be able to walk through. Inside the room was large and square with a high ceiling. It was essentially empty, the only two features being a green translucent plastic looking dome in the middle, about ten feet in diameter and some eight feet tall, plus dozens of white spheres the size of footballs evenly spaced throughout the room and each suspended by a single wire from the roof.

The walls, floor and ceiling were uniformly black, so the room was quite gloomy, with just enough light from the faintly glowing balls to allow safe movement. It did feel rather spooky though.

The Timekeeper joined his guest inside and began to wander towards the dome, so Alfred followed him. It was deathly quiet making the sounds of their steps echo clearly for the thirty seconds it took to reach the waiting dome, itself emitting a little illumination through its semi-opaque exterior.

There appeared to be no entrance. To Alfred's amazement the Timekeeper did not stop walking but instead continued right through the nearest arc of the wall and disappeared inside. Unsurprisingly the astonished youngster did not follow him, freezing in his tracks with eyes wide open. "What the …?"

After a few transfixed seconds the head of the Timekeeper eerily poked back out from the wall of the dome, looking surprised that his guest had not followed him into the peculiar structure. Realizing that what was perfectly natural for him was clearly very unnatural for the earthling, the Timekeeper moved fully out of the enclosure to offer some reassurance.

"I'm sorry, that was foolish of me. That must have been quite unsettling for you. Do not worry, the wall presents no physical obstruction and you can safely just walk right through it."

The originally spooky atmosphere had not been alleviated by this apparently ghost like ability to pass through what looked like a solid wall. Despite the encouragement of his host, this was not going to be an easy thing to do. Alfred's whole existence to this point had taught him that living people do not go through walls, and if they attempt to do so then the least they can expect is something of a bloody nose.

The Timekeeper calmly strolled over to the boy's side and turned back to face the dome. He could see just how much the recently earthbound human was struggling with this particular new experience and offered a suggestion. "How about you close your eyes and hold my hand on this occasion, then we can walk through together. I promise that you will not feel a thing."

Alfred looked up at the tall, pale faced alien and nodded without speaking. Then he squeezed his eyelids as tightly shut as they would go and held out his right hand, which the Timekeeper took before pulling him gently forward. Just a few seconds later the mini-ordeal was over as the tugging stopped to indicate that they were now inside. As promised there had been absolutely no sensation to betray the instant he had crossed the boundary.

"It's alright, you can open your eyes now."

# *Chapter Twenty-One*

In contrast to the outside space, the interior of the dome was very well lit with a bright pale green light that had no obvious source. It felt roomy enough since the only thing contained within was a central console; this had a waist high plinth supporting a large screen, plus a tilted panel sporting a keyboard along with quite a few switches, sliders and buttons. The screen was on and currently showing a view of the main room. There were no chairs or other furniture inside. There was what seemed to be a tall storage cupboard concealed behind a door.

The Timekeeper began to manipulate some of the controls, then typed several unrecognisable words. The camera view vanished, to be replaced by a plain blue background. None of the keys of the data entry board resembled characters familiar to the earthling, and there were at least twice as many as on a Standard English keyboard. After several seconds the screen changed once more, now showing what appeared to be an aerial shot of a large ancient city. The image was crystal clear, with enough visible movement of tiny figures to make it clear that it was not a photograph but more like a television picture.

"This is what we have selected for you as your first journey into a different era of time. The city that you can see is ancient Rome back on your home planet of Earth. It is actually quite a popular destination."

"Wow. I can't believe it. So, this is really ancient Rome rather than a simulation?"

"It is in no way a simulation. You are seeing reality as it was, and indeed still is in a sense."

Alfred could not speak for a minute as his poor overtaxed mind tried to deal with what he was being told. When he final managed to say something, it was only to confirm this state of disbelief and confusion. "I'm sorry, I mean this is wonderful, but I can barely take in what I am seeing, let alone fully understand it. I think that all I can do is simply accept what you are telling me, but not attempt to think about it too much for now."

"I understand. In a way we are being rather unfair dropping you straight into this, but after considerable discussion we felt that it was the right way to proceed. In any case, if it does all become too much, and you feel that you want to escape at any time, there is a safety word that you can use to quickly bring you back from the visited period. You will also be carefully monitored from the present and we will bring you back if we decide that it is appropriate to end the session ourselves. The safety word is TERMINATE."

"Well, I guess that makes me feel a little better. Most of me does actually want to do this and is excited about it. I wonder, is this then similar to when I visited Norros as a virtual character on my computer at home?"

"In a way, but also fundamentally different. You will not be a computer character here but yourself, one hundred percent you. And what you will be experiencing will be absolute reality, you will actually be immersed in the exact experience of time as it was. However, you will not be able to interact with anybody, no matter how real it may feel. The Time Telescope will be providing the reality of the space-time events that you experience, but the mechanisms of the Time Chamber will be continually augmenting that reality to make it feel like you are there rather than just seeing it. There is no real physical danger, however I warn you that your brain will find it almost impossible to accept that at times because of how realistic the experience is."

"OK, I am ready, I think. What happens next?"

"I will leave the room, and all that you need to do is wait here. It will take roughly an earth minute for the Telescope to engage and transfer the relevant space-time location into the main room. You will actually see the image forming and focusing as you wait, but please stay within the dome until the internal lighting changes from green to amber. After that just step outside into ancient Rome at your leisure. As you are obviously not used to it the experience will seem very strange to begin with. You will be able to see the dome once outside, and this will be your normal means of entry and exit from your selected destination. I suggest, for your own reassurance, that you do not stray too far from the dome to begin with, and feel free to step back inside for a moment whenever you want to. There is no limit to the duration of your excursion into the past, but I suggest no more than an hour. When you decide that you have had enough on this occasion, return into the dome and push this large green button here to end the session, which again takes roughly a minute. I will then come and collect you."

Alfred looked at the green button, a hemisphere about the size of half an apple. Beside it was a similarly shaped button coloured red. "That all sounds fairly straight forward. Thank you for the clear explanation."

"You are welcome. Oh, one more thing – the cupboard over there contains a toilet for your comfort should you need it."

Alfred laughed. "You know I had been wondering about that particular issue, especially since I am very nervous, and that does tend to have a relevant effect upon the human body. Thank you so much for providing such a vital facility."

The Timekeeper responded with his own subdued laughter. "I assure you that it is not just humans who suffer from such an issue. This is a very simple form of experience room. There are others that are much larger and more sophisticated, where researchers can spend extended periods in other space-time locations. The facilities available there are correspondingly more comprehensive and complex, and the degree of augmentation can also be much greater." He paused for a moment, then smiled. "Anyway, I shall now leave you to it. Just relax and enjoy your visit."

With that the Timekeeper pressed the red button and abruptly disappeared through the wall of the dome, leaving his guest suddenly feeling a lot more anxious at the prospect of what was about to happen.

The monitor screen went blank, and Alfred could just hear the faint steps of his departing host, followed by the sound of the outside door to experience room fourteen closing, and then complete silence. The young earthling began to feel a rush of adrenalin making his whole body tremble. He knew that something amazing must be happening outside the dome, yet there was no physical sensation of this for the first twenty seconds, until a perceptible confused noise began to seep in from beyond the strange internal walls. It gradually grew louder but no less incomprehensible, becoming a little uncomfortable until it suddenly dissolved into a still very audible but now crystal-clear cacophony of sounds of people talking and moving about. A few seconds later the light inside the dome switched from pale green to amber to announce that the Time Telescope had completed its task of generating a slice of first century Rome. The mixed male and female voices were unmistakably speaking fluent Latin, not that Alfred had any expertise in that classic tongue, but he could at least tell that it was indeed Latin.

Now he had to gather himself and step outside the shelter of the dome. This was difficult enough, even without knowledge of what lay beyond, since he was still rather phased by the idea of walking through an apparently solid wall. It took fully another minute before he could just about summon the courage to exit the structure. He strolled over to the barrier, closed his eyes, and then leapt forwards.

Slowly he reopened them, but before this the first thing he noticed was that it felt noticeably much hotter, and the light was very bright even through his shut eyelids. Instinctively he held his right hand above his forehead to provide a screen before opening them.

He continued with opening his eyes until they were as fully open as they could physically have become. It was the most unbelievable scene that he had ever seen, and that included some pretty amazing recent sights. This was not a movie, or a computer game. He was really standing in a smoothly cobbled thoroughfare in the magnificent classical city of ancient Rome. The most telling indicator that this was no illusion but instead the real thing was the smell, which to be honest could have been sweeter. The unmistakeable aroma of manure filtered through his nostrils, making him grimace for a moment. Unsurprisingly, there were several instances of the source of the olfactory pollution on display as several horses wandered in both directions, some with riders and some pulling carts. The street seemed to be quite busy, with a highly positioned sun announcing the time to be close to midday.

There were two storey stone buildings lining the road in a continuous terrace structure, however not far ahead the route opened out into a far more spacious area with an ornamental fountain and some distance beyond that a smattering of much larger buildings.

The fifty or so citizens currently in view did not seem to be aware of his presence. He was not sure what would happen if any of them accidently barged into his small body but resolved to try not to let this happen anyway. To assist with that he decided to make his way without delay to the open area, whilst taking in the immediate surroundings as he walked.

The tactile experience was completely realistic. He had to be a little careful traversing the perceptible solid mounds of the cobble stones, although they were at least smooth and level enough not to provide too much obstruction, particularly to the wooden wheels of the half dozen carts, most of which seemed laden with foodstuffs as if on their way to local markets. Alfred could even feel a gentle breeze brushing past his cheeks.

So far it was not an unpleasant introduction to visiting the past. This did feel absolutely like genuine time travel, even if the Timekeeper had stated that technically it was not, since he could only see the past without actually being able to change either it or subsequent events that followed on from the occasion. Of course, he only had the most rudimentary understanding of what was going on, though kind of felt that he had got the gist of it.

He was quickly warming to the experience, quite literally because of the decidedly Mediterranean climate. The temperature must have been above thirty degrees, something that he was definitely not accustomed to. If he had known he would certainly have brought some sun cream lotion to splash on, and his mother would undoubtedly not be pleased to hear of him venturing out into such searing heat without a liberal screen of the liquid protection. What would he do if he got a suntan? How on earth would he explain that? Could he even get a suntan, or worse still sunburn? Oh dear, this was all very weird, and got more confusing the more he thought about it.

The predominantly male roman citizens were dressed just as he might have expected, in short togas that were generally of earthy colours or a rather drab shade of red. They were generally not that tall for adults, certainly not by twentieth century standards, and there was little sign of any excess fat on their fit looking bodies. There were just a couple of women on view, quite young looking, wearing longish plain white dresses that dropped almost down to their ankles. Their shoulder length dark hair was partially braided towards the front edges, and both carried small brown leather bags slung diagonally across their slim frames.

Many of the open windows of the upper story of the houses along the passageway had various garments hanging over the ledges, presumably to dry them after having recently been washed. An old woman's head poked out from one of the apertures, staring down at the passers-by, as though remembering long gone days when she had been as young as they. Alfred felt a little sad for her, then remembered that she had been dead for two thousand years. That realisation did not help much though, and he continued to feel sorry for her; it was remarkably difficult to accept that what he was seeing was not real. The paradox was a result of the fact that in a way this was real. The Time Telescope was watching reality as it was, because in one sense that reality still existed.

Completely bemused, the schoolboy was tempted to give his face a quick slap to try and bring him out of the state of mental chaos that the temporal confusion had led his brain into. Sidereal had warned him that sometimes it would be vital to stop trying to figure things out, and just take a step back to avoid going crazy. This was clearly one of those moments. Accept where and when he was for now, and just enjoy the experience.

The large open public area was now upon him, allowing the novice time tourist to see everything within and surrounding it. The two most notable things on the neatly paved surface were a small market to the right, and a group of parading soldiers formed up on the left-hand side. The legionnaires were closest, so he tentatively moved nearer to inspect them. His caution was more to do with their intimidating appearance rather than actual fear of coming to any harm, which he knew should not be possible.

There were about a hundred of the military men. Out in front stood a single officer wearing a red cloak, and Alfred recalled from his history lessons at Lime Lane Primary that this was typical for the roman army, with each such unit commanded by a centurion. That matched up with the English word "century" meaning a hundred, which had been derived from the old Latin language. The troops were short in stature, however their bare arms and legs looked very muscular; they clearly represented a fearsome opponent to any who dared to stand in their way. The ordinary rank and file wore a sort of banded armour around their torsos, and each was armed with a short sword in a scabbard hanging from their waists, along with a strange spear that had a wooden stock tipped by a menacing metal shank and sharp point. Protection came from a large rectangular shield held in their left arms. The centurion bore no spear and carried a distinctive oval shield.

The sight was quite engrossing. Alfred would not have minded hanging round to observe them further, however the sun was quite fierce making him keen to move on and perhaps find some shade. The market stalls offered such a prospect, so he turned and made his way over to them, at the same time perusing the surrounding buildings.

The most impressive of these was on the far side directly opposite the passage he had entered the open area from. It looked very much like some Government building rather than a private house, seeming far too large for the latter purpose. The frontage was adorned with a row of ten thick pure white pillars holding up an enormous overhanging porch. There were a dozen extremely wide steps leading up to a high and wide entrance. Several official looking people dressed in long white togas were milling around at various levels of the steps, as though they were waiting to go inside, or had just come out from some meeting. On top of the building was a huge dome, again in white but with a smaller hemisphere at the top that was decorated with a shiny silver coating. There were elaborate carvings on the face of the porch and at various places around the lower roof. At the base of the steps was a spectacular chariot with four white horses standing patiently in colourful traces.

As Alfred reached the first of the market stalls he could now make out the conversations of some of the traders and customers. To begin with he could not understand a word of what they were saying since it was all in Latin, a language that he was only vaguely familiar with. His personal vocabulary of the ancient form of Italian was limited to barely a dozen words and phrases that had been absorbed into modern day usage, such as 'ad infinitum' and 'et tu Brute' from Shakespeare's play chronicling the demise of Julius Caesar. After a few seconds though he was astonished to realise that they were suddenly now speaking in fluent English. Quickly he guessed that it must be the amazing processing technology incorporated into the

Telescope that was translating the spoken words in real time so that he could understand what was being said. Grateful for this remarkable assistance, he listened to the verbal exchanges of the ancient roman citizens.

"No, that is too expensive."

"I'm sorry, but there is a shortage at the moment. There have been delays in the galleys getting here from Egypt that has pushed up the prices that I must pay at the docks. I have no choice but to pass on the extra cost."

"Do you know what is causing the delays?"

"They tell me that they have been having to take a longer route to avoid raids by pirates."

"Not those damn Phoenicians again. Why doesn't the Government do something about it?"

"I wish they would. But right now, I still have to put my prices up."

"Oh, very well. I shall take six please."

Finally, the male trader and female shopper concluded their contract with the exchange of three coins for six large vegetables of a type that Alfred did not recognise. It was not quite Tesco's, but the increasing prices sounded all too familiar and contemporary.

The trader's stall was very neatly laid out, with perhaps fifty different products including many bowls of what looked and smelt like spices. There were some thirty different stalls in total, well-spaced and arranged in no particularly geometric pattern. About half were selling foodstuffs, with the rest mainly vending clothes, raw fabrics, carpets and basic pottery for everyday domestic use. There was one though that seemed especially interesting.

Standing behind a couple of broad tables was a very tall seller with extremely black skin and a broad attractive grin formed by a set of perfect teeth. His stall presented a large number of what were clearly artistic creations, mainly paintings interspersed by a few sculptures. All were of a surprisingly high standard, unexpected because Alfred was not aware that such artistic expertise existed in this era. Not that he was very clued up in the subject.

The tall trader was slim yet extremely muscular and did not give the appearance of being a typical artist in this respect. He also looked a little out of place since he was obviously of African origin. The twentieth century schoolboy wondered how the talented foreigner had come to be living in the ancient roman capital. As he scrutinised the different artworks he spotted a clue in the common theme of many of them, which clearly depicted gladiatorial scenes of men fighting in the arena. Thankfully they were somewhat sanitised images without any blood or gore. One of the paintings had two battling combatants, one of whom looked remarkably like the powerfully built merchant. It seemed, given this evidence and his physique, that the friendly looking artist must have once been a gladiator himself. Alfred remembered that some very capable and successful gladiators were ultimately given their freedom as a reward for there gruesome compulsory efforts; his conclusion was that this was a good example of someone who had survived the many battles forced upon him long enough to be granted his liberty and made a full roman citizen.

Alfred was thankful that the man had escaped from such a terrible profession, and that he had gained the opportunity to show off what in his humble opinion was a far worthier outlet for the man's true talents. He so admired the ex-fighter's work that he would have loved to have been able to purchase one of the smaller paintings. It was a great pity that such a transaction was not possible, and perhaps an even greater pity that this impressive portfolio was probably by the commencement of his own millennium lost to the ravages of time.

Turning to investigate some of the remaining stalls, Alfred started to feel a little thirsty. The hot climate was definitely something that he was not used to. He could not even remember a single summer's day back in his home town that came close to this. It was nice to experience for a short spell, or even a couple of weeks holiday, but permanent heat like this was too much for an English schoolboy more used to cool and damp conditions.

One table right at the end of the row of flimsy shops was packed with a couple of dozen earthenware vessels that seemed to contain products for drinking, as evidenced by the vendor who was pouring out some red liquid into a jug belonging to a female shopper. Alfred guessed that it must be wine since he knew that to be a popular drink with people of the time. He was not personally a fan of the alcoholic beverage, having only tasted a tiny mouthful of it once before under close supervision, when he had come to the conclusion that he much preferred lemonade.

Whether there was anything suitable for his own tastes in one of the other containers was a moot point, although he could not help wondering what would happen if he were to discretely try to take a sip of something. Thus far he had not really touched anything apart from the ground that he was walking on. It was surely now appropriate to test this world further by attempting to physically interact with it a bit more. Carefully he held out his hand and touched the top of the table with his index finger. It felt solid, so he pressed his palm against the wooden surface. Yes, definitely solid. Now to try one of the fired clay vessels. Once more there was positive resistance to his prodding finger.

It was by now obvious that this was a very real reality rather than just an image of the ancient city. This was becoming confusing again, since he had been briefed that he could not alter events by his presence. Perhaps he had misunderstood and had instead been told that he should not alter events even if technically he could. What would happen if he tried to push one of the relatively fragile vessels off the table to see if it would fall onto the hard floor below and shatter?

He knew that he did not dare to perform any such practical experiment; he certainly did not want to upset the Timekeeper or anyone else at the fascinating Historical Ministry. Clarification would have to be sought through verbal enquiry once back in normal time. Except that of course normal time was still not normal time as he was still existing out of time compared to everyone that he knew back on Earth. This was getting ridiculous.

It seemed a clear signal that perhaps it was time to bring to an end his first excursion into the distant past. The Government building on the far side of the open public space still stood invitingly close by, and part of him was aching to go and take a look inside. Regrettably, he knew that it would have to wait until a future trip into the annals of the past.

The short journey back to the dome that provided the base for his temporal jaunt only took five minutes. Closing his eyes upon reaching the boundary he gratefully jumped through it. Inside, the clear green button to terminate the incredible experience beckoned, and he pushed it without further delay or ceremony.

# Chapter Twenty-Two

There was little time, ironically, to dwell any longer in experience room fourteen. Alfred did feel, however, that once he got more used to the weirdness of it all then he could comfortably spend a good few hours there without a break. It was intoxicating, and it made his history lessons at school, which he had hitherto been very enthusiastic about, suddenly seem pedestrian and by comparison rather dull. That was no fault of his dedicated teacher, but how could Lime Lane Primary possibly compete with this?

After a minute he jumped out into the main area to see that it had now fully returned to the dimly lit emptiness of its non-operational state. The sensation of being in the first century then instantaneously returning to the twenty-first century was very unsettling, so it took him a few seconds to readjust to normality, however he then realised that this was still very far from normality. It suddenly became difficult to comprehend what was real, and his head started spinning, making him feel a little dizzy and nauseous.

Sidereal must have anticipated this as the door to the chamber clicked and swung open to allow the young alien to enter carrying a glass of pale green liquid as he strode towards his compatriot.

"Here, drink this. It will help you feel better."

The earthling's new friend put his free arm on the wobbly youngster's shoulder as he passed him the clear glass cup. Alfred was still thirsty from the heat of ancient Rome so was very grateful to receive it. He slowly sipped the cold, refreshing liquid, his eyes opening gradually wider with each gulp.

"Hmm, that is nice." After a few seconds he did indeed start to feel a lot less queasy and much steadier on his feet. "Wow, what is this? I feel quite alright now."

"It is water with a little juice from a berry that grows in the gardens outside the refectory of the Grand Library. I guess the mixture is what you on Earth would call a pick-me-up."

"Well it certainly works. I was starting to go faint. Sorry about that."

"No please, don't worry at all. Most people feel disoriented the first time they finish a session in one of the experience rooms. When you consider that you have sort of been sent back in time then perhaps it is really not so surprising to feel peculiar about it."

"I see your point. It is just such an astonishing feeling. Truly breath-taking. I suppose the only thing better would be to really travel back in time and be able to interact with the past and people from ancient times."

"Hey, slow down my friend." Sidereal laughed as he reigned in the over-enthusiasm of the pupil from modern England. "Seeing the past is all that is in your curriculum for now. Anything else that may or may not be possible you will have to bide your time over."

The Timekeeper entered the room and came over to join them. Despite being abruptly pulled up, Alfred but could not help looking very pleased at the mere suggestion that more might be possible. "Sorry, I am more than thankful for what I have already been able to do, and you are quite right, I don't think I could cope with anything more just now. I did get confused about a few things, but I think I shall save any questions for later. May I thank you, Timekeeper, and all the staff here for letting me do this. Thank you so much."

"Our pleasure, Master Alfred," responded the Historical Ministry official.

Sidereal retrieved the now half empty glass, taking a quick sip himself, and the three of them then made their way out into the corridor and then along back to the lounge with the welcome assistance of the marvellous metallic flying mat. Alfred sat on one of the comfortable sofas, glad of the opportunity to relax for a moment.

"So, how was ancient Rome?" asked the venerable chief of the Time Telescope enthusiastically, exuding undisguised pride in the complex machinery.

"Amazing. I cannot find the words to describe my feelings." Alfred turned to look at Sidereal. "How was your own experience?"

"Fascinating. I went for a quick trip back to third century BC Athens. Very beautiful, and very civilised".

"Sounds good. Glad you enjoyed it. I look forward to visiting the place myself. Imagine running into somebody like Archimedes. That would just be too much. You didn't run into Archimedes, did you?"

"No. I was just sitting admiring the view from the Parthenon, watching the Greek citizens go about their daily business."

"The Parthenon? Wow. I've seen photographs of it, but I understand that it is not much more than a shell nowadays. And you were sitting there seeing it in all its ancient glory." It was impossible to conceal his excitement, to the point where the Timekeeper decided it might be prudent to try and calm the youngster down a little.

"I am overjoyed by your interest in history, and I am confident that you will be able to visit us again, when you will be more than welcome. I think now though we should be getting you back to the library for a rest. This is all very new for you, and way beyond what you are psychologically used to. We must be careful not too push your young mind too far too quickly."

"You are right, of course, sir. I am feeling very strange right now. It is a good feeling, but my brain is quite mixed up. A cup of tea and a lie down sounds like a really good idea."

# *Chapter Twenty-Three*

Kriosta was waiting for his pupil at the nearest train stop to the library, where Alfred had earlier departed for the Historical Ministry. Sidereal had accompanied him on the return journey, but now bade him a temporary farewell as he was going to visit a friend living in the surrounding city. It was early afternoon with a few hours to spare before the scheduled evening meal, so Alfred's tutor suggested that they too take a walk through the city streets on their way back and grab a snack in a favourite café of his. By now the youngster was feeling quite peckish so was more than happy to agree to that suggestion.

The sprawling urban conurbation was generally well spaced out with wide roads and plenty of green spaces, along with paved plazas where people could sit out in the open. Their present path though was taking them in the direction of what appeared to be an older part of town, where the buildings not only looked quite antiquated but were by contrast packed quite tightly together, separated by narrow lanes. Most of the buildings seemed to be living quarters, but there were a few shops, their Victorian facades resembling those he had seen on Norros, plus as promised a few cafes and restaurants along with what looked like an inn.

There were not so many people about at present. As they reached the little refreshment establishment chosen by his tutor it was clear to Alfred that plenty of others likewise held it in high regard since it was almost full of customers, comfortably a couple of dozen. Fortunately, there was a single table with two chairs still vacant, so they squeezed through to claim it.

There did not appear to be any staff, or even a counter where they could go to place an order. Spotting his ward's look of confusion, Kriosta waved his right paw across the surface of the table, and instantly two large virtual menus sprang up into view, one before each of them. They seemed to display CUET like sensitivity to the needs of the individual, with Alfred's electronic card customised to show a large list of the sort of food and drinks that definitely appealed to him. He could not help grinning with delight and shaking his head in amazement.

"Unbelievable. How do I make a selection?"

"Touch choice with finger."

"Thank you. Let's see. It's close to three o'clock, so I guess I shall go for a pot of afternoon tea, a warm cheese and onion pasty, since my mum is not here to tell me off, and a strawberry scone with clotted cream for exactly the same reason. How about you, sir."

"Kriosta try same."

The alien had already learnt that anything his young friend ordered was likely to taste nice, so decided it would be a good idea to copy him. He waved his paw again and the menus vanished with the same rapidity that they had appeared.

"It just occurred to me, sir, how do we pay?"

"Not need pay. All free here. On house."

"Really? I am starting to like this place. I may decide not to go back to Earth!"

Kriosta looked startled for a moment, until he realised that Alfred was only joking.

The earthling sat back in his chair to patiently wait for the order to arrive. He assumed that some staff member would finally show their face to carry it over to the table. As was all too common when away from his home world, he could not have been more wrong. After about two minutes a small section of wall nearby slid open and a silver tray loaded with their choice of food and drink flew slowly out and steered towards their table, hovering momentarily above it and then gently lowering itself onto the surface.

"Well, I suppose at least we won't need to leave a tip."

The pair tucked into their concise meal, with Kriosta enthusiastically devouring both pasty and scone with a flourish of his long pink tongue, and Alfred showing more characteristic restraint as befitted his English manners.

"Good choice," commented Kriosta with an approving smile.

"Indeed," replied Alfred, still eating his own scone.

A man and woman on another table got up and left, the respective tray subsequently rising and heading for the opening in the wall in a show of extreme extra-terrestrial efficiency. The remaining customers continued eating and chatting in a low voice. There was not a mobile phone in sight. The schoolboy reflected upon the contrast with the typical twenty-first century eatery back home, where civilised behaviour now seemed at a premium, and where ear defenders were becoming an essential accessory along with the more traditional knives and forks.

The visitors were now sipping their tea. Kriosta often struggled with the handles of cups so was grasping his drinking vessel in both paws as he raised it to his snout.

"Sir," inquired Alfred, "Have you ever used the Time Telescope yourself?"

"Yes. Used much. Sometimes Earth history. Sometimes other planets. Sometimes own planet."

"You have visited Earth's past? That's interesting. Any particular periods?"

"Ancient Egypt. Much like. Like pyramids."

"Oh, I wish I go could and visit them, either in the present or the past." Something in the depths of Alfred's brain seemed to hint that maybe there was more to his tutor's visit than the interest of a tourist. He felt compelled to ask a further question without really knowing quite why. "Any particular reason for choosing that time and location?"

The generally open and forthcoming alien did not immediately reply, instead looking slightly uncomfortable with the nominally innocent inquiry. He appeared to try and stall for time by taking a big gulp of tea whilst searching for a suitable answer. Alfred felt a smidgeon of guilt at having asked what was perhaps an indiscreet question, yet he was also now very intrigued.

"Kriosta not lie. Yes. Can say not more. Secret. Very secret. Much sorry."

"Fair enough. I won't ask any more about it, but I am now even more curious, so if you ever decide that you can tell me more then please do so."

"Agree."

A few more people left. Alfred was quite happy to stay for the moment. He was tempted to request the menu again, although guilt got the better of him so refrained from doing so. The very nice refreshments already consumed would do for now. There was still some tea left in his pot and he used this to top up his cup, then did the same for his tutor also.

"Something else I wondered about, if you don't mind me asking, is whether you were ever a student at the library yourself? I mean, when you were younger."

"Yes. When younger. Many times since. Never too old learn. Many, many things left learn."

"I guess that is true. Back on Earth most people learn while they are still at school and then don't ever really study again. I suppose they are too busy working and just trying to get by to have time to go back to school."

"Great pity."

"For sure. Did you have any favourite subjects?"

"Love science."

"Me too. Especially anything to do with space. The universe is an amazing place, and I love watching documentaries about how it all works. Things like black holes, supernovae and the big bang."

"Big bang?"

"Yes. You know, how the universe came into being. How it started from a single point and then suddenly expanded."

"Understand now. Entropy cause."

"Excuse me?"

"Entropy cause. Relationship between two types entropy."

"Er, I don't follow. I have heard of entropy, but I did not realise there were two types. What do you mean, sir?"

"Very simple. Two types entropy. Thermodynamic. Also Statistical. Third law thermodynamics states entropy always increase. Never decrease. If increases then statistical entropy must also increase. Statistical linked to volume, so volume must increase. So, Big Bang starts increase in volume. Relationship thermodynamic to statistical entropy mean universe continue rapid expand. Simple."

Alfred sat back looking slightly gobsmacked. "Er, sir, I am young and no expert on cosmology, even by earth standards, but it suddenly occurs to me that your understanding of physics is bound to be far greater than any humans. That places me in an awkward situation. Normally it would take me many, many years to learn what the cleverest humans know about the universe. Then, maybe if I turned out to be clever myself I might one day add to that knowledge in a small way. If I turned out to be another Einstein, which personally I consider to be highly unlikely, then I might even make some ground-breaking discovery and win a Nobel Prize. But now, just by chattng to you, I have learnt something that no other human has yet figured out."

"Master Alfred already know many things no other human know."

"Well, yes, that's true. But in this case, it seems different to me. I do not feel at all comfortable about the specific issue of being told things about physics that great scientists, who have devoted their entire lives trying to understand, have not yet discovered themselves. It just does not seem right and fair."

His tutor lowered his eyes and thought carefully for a dozen seconds. "Kriosta understand. Think Magister agree. Kriosta be careful what say. Master Alfred very wise and good."

"I'm slowly learning, and I also have a very good tutor."

Taking a final sip Kriosta stood up and went around to put his paws on Alfred's shoulders. The youngster finished off the dregs of his own cup and stood up too.

"We leave now. Walk back through library gardens."

With that they exited the café, the tray on their table leaping into the air and out of sight as they opened the door. Outside they strolled through the buildings until they reached a very wide road that separated the older zone from the magnificent gardens of the Grand Library, its central golden dome gleaming in the still bright artificially enhanced sunlight. There was no traffic at all, which was surprising to the earthling, used as he was to residing in the overcrowded streets of modern Britain where the car was almost as prevalent as the citizens. It appeared that people here were more than happy to walk everywhere by default, or take the train for longer excursions. No bad thing, to be honest, thought Alfred.

# *Chapter Twenty-Four*

The gardens were very pleasant to wander through, aided by a copious positioning of benches to sit and rest on. There were quite a few students taking advantage of these to read in solitude amidst the green lawns and flower beds. Slightly unexpected was the fact that most clasped physical copies of real books and manuscripts rather than digital versions on hand held electronic readers. It was pleasing to see this preference for the more tactile experience.

Arguably the most attractive feature of the gardens was the sizeable lake more or less in the middle of the landward side. There were waterfowl gliding around the surface, and some small boats slowly manoeuvring about, without oars it should be said, implying a more futuristic and subtle propulsion system. There was something to be said for the old-fashioned system, Alfred reckoned, if only to burn off the odd calorie.

As he slowly accompanied his tutor around the edge of the giant pond he spotted something about a hundred metres further along the circumference that looked surprisingly familiar. He was not certain at this range, however the flowing golden hairstyle of what was undoubtedly a woman did look ever so familiar. Could it be? Straining his eyes to the limit could not provide confirmation, so he quickened his pace in anticipation. By the time he had closed the gap to a mere fifty metres he had eliminated any remaining doubt.

"Sir, it's the Princess. I don't believe it. What is she doing here, and how did she get here?"

He was sorely tempted to shout out her name, but did not wish to disturb the tranquillity, so waited until he had almost reached her before quietly exclaiming, "Your Highness, is it really you?"

The lady had been engrossed reading a book and had not noticed him, but upon hearing his voice she raised her head enthusiastically. "Alfred, how wonderful it is to meet you again."

"Likewise, your Highness. Well, you never know who you are going to bump into in the galaxy".

Marlena giggled. She was clearly happy to be visiting the library. "Definitely true."

"Any particular reason for being here?"

The question was heavily loaded, as Alfred realised this must be more than mere coincidence.

"Since you mention it, yes. The Magister invited me. He had planned for you to visit a certain planet tomorrow that is a particular favourite of mine, so he knew that I would be interested in tagging along."

"Terrific. By the way, may I ask how you got here so quickly?"

"You may. We Martians have our own interplanetary transport, but it is not so fast, relatively speaking of course. I think NASA would be more than happy with it, however it would have taken forever to get to the library using our own spaceship. Fortunately, we have access to a machine loaned to us by the good people of Olympus"

"Olympus? You mean as in the Greek gods? Are you friends with Zeus?"

"Not exactly. I did mention it briefly before, you might recall. There is a reclusive world on the very outer rim of the galaxy that is by far the oldest and most advanced civilisation known to us. We call it Olympus in English purely because in a way there are some parallels, although we certainly do not consider them to be gods. They are very mysterious, however, and tend to keep themselves to themselves. They are a good and kind race, and it is very nice of them to help out by lending us some transport that can make the journey in next to no time."

"Wow. Is it something similar to the technology used in my tutor's spaceship?"

The Princess paused and looked up at the standing figure of Kriosta, smiling in admiration. "I can't really discuss that, although you might be surprised to learn that our furry friend is held in the highest regard by the Olympians and is one of the very few people to have visited the fabled Old Palace on their planet. On that basis, you can imagine that he may have benefited from that relationship with respect to his wonderful old machine."

It was Alfred's turn to stare admiringly at his tutor. "I guess I should not be too shocked to hear about that. I always suspected there was far more to him than meets the eye."

The modest alien looked embarrassed, looking straight down at the ground without speaking. Alfred patted him on the arm to try and alleviate his discomfort. "I am very lucky to have you by my side, sir. Believe me, I know that."

"Kriosta lucky know Master Alfred. Lucky know Princess."

Having established everyone's good fortune, Alfred was now curious about what Marlena had said regarding the following day's activities. "Your Highness, can you tell me more about what they have planned for me tomorrow? What is that planet that you mentioned?"

"It is not so far away and is very large, with a naturally wide variety of different environments. Such conditions made it the perfect place to establish what it now serves as, a huge conservation world. The staff there manage it in addition to monitoring other planets throughout the galaxy to look for species that are in danger of becoming extinct."

"I see. That sounds really wonderful. And I understand now why you want to go there. I know that the natural world means a great deal to you."

"More than you can know, Alfred. Before the great disaster on Mars my own planet was very beautiful and contained other species than ours. They were all lost in the cataclysm. Although it was before my time, the surviving records tell of these creatures. It made me appreciate even more the natural environment on Earth, and the amazing variety of life there. What has happened during the last hundred years has greatly saddened me. Many times I have cried over the terrible toll taken by the rise of humanity. At least, when I become so sad, I can console myself by visiting the conservation world and seeing the results of their marvellous efforts to at least mitigate some of the damage."

"I understand your sadness, so I also share your enthusiasm for the idea of this conservation world. If that is my next destination, then I am very pleased about that and looking forward to going there."

The Princess had temporarily lost her cheerful demeanour, but it now returned with a flash of her perfect teeth. "Good for you, Alfred. Why don't we head on back to the library for a coffee?"

"Sounds good to me."

With a flick of her hair the royal lady stood up and the three of them began a leisurely stroll around to the other side of the lake, where it met with the main path that led to the rear entrance of the library. It was still quite bright and warm, prompting the Martian to take out her floppy hat from the large shoulder bag that she was carrying and plonk it upon her head. The accumulated dosage of centuries of ultra-violet rays had not aged her skin one bit, so it was more an instrument of comfort than protection from any prospect of sunburn. It did in any case really suit her.

Maybe it was the complete absence of pollution, but Alfred could clearly smell a multitude of different aromas from the many beautiful flower beds decorating either side of the thoroughfare. It was quite invigorating, almost overpowering his little nose at times. He noticed the occasional twitching of his tutor's long and far more sensitive snout. It also seemed to impart a suspiciously pleasant feeling of well being that might well have rendered the responsible flora borderline illegal back in his home country.

Soon the trio found themselves crossing the pretty bridge that traversed the final obstacle on the route to the famous, magnificent building, where they paused briefly to admire the architecture. Moving off again they quickly gained the highest level of the terraces, where they sat down at a round white table with four chairs. An attendant came over and kindly offered to bring them a tray of beverages and biscuits.

The area was sparsely populated at the moment, in contrast to the crowd that had occupied it at the time of the earthling's first arrival. Perhaps most people were in lessons or down reading in the library vaults.

Just then Grattin appeared in the main entrance door, and after spotting the group made his way over to join them, sitting down on the spare chair. "Hello everyone. I hope you are all well and enjoying yourselves."

"Yes, sir, thank you. I must admit I have not yet quite got over my temporal exploration experience using the Time Telescope. It was wonderful. To walk around the streets of ancient Rome was beyond exhilarating. It is one thing to read about it in books, or see a reconstruction in the movies, but that was the real thing. I cannot even begin to imagine the implications of having access to such a machine."

"You are quite right, Master Alfred. The implications are enormous. For example, in the area of law and justice. Not so much for us, as crime is virtually non-exist on most developed worlds in the galaxy. But imagine if the police back on Earth could view the past in absolutely accurate detail. Nobody would be able to commit any crime and expect to get away with it."

"My goodness, I hadn't thought of that. I guess it might take some of the fun, if that is the correct word, out of the great conspiracy theories of Earth's past. We could finally see if there really was a man behind the grassy knoll when President John F Kennedy was assassinated."

Kriosta looked puzzled by the reference, although the other two aliens understood.

"And what happened to Glenn Miller," added the Princess.

"And why the dinosaurs became extinct. Actually, I could go back and see some real dinosaurs, at least if I was brave enough, which I probably wouldn't be if I was being honest."

"Sorry to disappoint you," countered the Magister, "but that is not currently possible. The way the telescope works is to read the residual traces of time that still exist in the present. Without going into detail, contrary to what people on Earth believe time is not instantaneous but persistent. Space-Time events are created and then decay, somewhat ironically, over time. That means that historical events become more and more difficult to read the longer ago they occurred. Obviously in the case of the dinosaurs we are talking about more than fifty million years ago, and unfortunately the Time Telescope is simply not sensitive enough to pick out enough temporal detail that can then be processed. I should say that it is not sensitive enough yet. Our scientists at the Historical Ministry are constantly working to improve the sensitivity of the receiver, so don't give up hope of being able to come face to face with a Tyrannosaurus Rex one day."

"I sort of understand, except for that bit about the persistence of time. Sorry, I get frustrated by my lack of knowledge of physics sometimes."

"Please, you are only ten years old. For a human child your knowledge is in fact very impressive. Within a decade you will be very good at physics, I think. Be patient."

"Thank you. I will try to be."

The attendant reappeared to bring the Magister a coffee, which he gratefully took a gulp of. "You know, Alfred, despite the animosity felt by many in the galaxy towards humans for the way they have abused their environment, there is at the same time an enormous admiration for human culture. You will have noticed that quite a lot of that culture had been imported, and two of the most popular products are your twin beverages of tea and coffee. And I should definitely add biscuits to that list as well. Especially the sheer variety of biscuits. Delicious."

"You're very welcome."

"We also love your films, television, music and literature."

"Absolutely," chipped in Marlena. "And don't forget art. Speaking as a purely amateur painter, I adore the work of the great human artists."

"Do you have a favourite?" asked Alfred.

"Well, I have to admit to having a soft spot for Leonardo da Vinci. But then again, I did have the privilege of meeting him once."

"What? Seriously?" exclaimed the astonished schoolboy.

"Yes. Even got to shake his hand. Believe it or not he was working on the Mona Lisa at the time. Charming young lady who modelled for him. I spent quite a few years living in Italy around that time."

"You are amazing, your Highness. I am lost for words."

"As Grattin said, there is much about humanity to admire, and my long lifespan has given me the chance to experience a lot of it first-hand. I am very fortunate in that respect. On the other hand, I have also had to witness the bad side of your species as well. The wars, the terrible tragedies, and the cruelty of so many. And of course, the horrible treatment of animals and the destruction of your beautiful natural world."

There followed a break in the conversation as they recognised the dark direction it had moved in. The Magister finally decided to restore the mood a little. "On that point, can I let you know, if you did not know already, what is happening tomorrow. We will be visiting the giant conservation planet of Agreether."

"Yes," said the Princess, "we did mention it to Alfred. We are all really looking forward to going there."

"Excellent. I have spoken to the people that run the conservation program, so they will be expecting you. Kriosta, I would be grateful if you would travel there using your spaceship, and land at the main headquarters building just outside the grounds of the reserve."

"Understand. Agree."

"Thank you. I should just give you a few more details, Alfred, about the place you will be visiting. It is divided up into many zones each containing a variety of creatures grouped together by planet of origin or native environment. There is a zone primarily dedicated to wildlife from Earth. You might be interested to learn that much of that conservation work was done with the help of the Princess and her fellow Martians, which was not an easy task, so all credit to them for their efforts. The zones, as well as the entire outer boundary of the reserve, are separated by force fields. They are there purely to keep the animals in the correct location rather than as a protective measure. However, be careful to avoid touching the force field as it will give you a mildly uncomfortable jolt. There are some places containing dangerous and fierce creatures, although you will be carefully sheperded by the staff working in the reserve, so hopefully you will not get eaten."

Alfred was not entirely sure that the Magister was joking about him being a potential meal. "Hopefully not, sir".

"Anyway, it will be quite an intensive day tomorrow, so I suggest that you all relax for the rest of the day. I have to head back to my office now, but I look forward to seeing you all at dinner this evening."

# *Chapter Twenty-Five*

There was no way of saying it diplomatically. Much as he liked his home town in England, back on Earth, the weather there was generally awful. It did make the nice sunny days all the more welcome when he could go out for walks with his mother. Here though, at the main headquarters on this wonderful giant alien world, the climate was unerringly gorgeous. The very large star that the planet orbited played a large part in the utopian environment, but this was also augmented by a sophisticated meteorological control system powered by numerous fusion reactors spread around the surface of the globe. Indeed, much of the work had been dedicated towards introducing a seasonal element to the conditions for the benefit of the large number of creatures housed on the conservation world. There was even an artic like zone located at the northern pole, that being the coolest area on a long-term natural basis, although that still meant well above zero degrees without intervention. Unexpectedly, the lowest temperature was almost one hundred degrees below the freezing point of water, where the incumbents were obviously not indigenous to the planet Earth.

Conversely the hottest temperature, at the southern pole, was boosted to near the boiling point of water to cater for the extraordinary creatures housed there. Most of the surface however tended towards a normal temperature of twenty-five degrees at noon falling to about half that during the night.

Alfred was most keen, in an understandably partisan way, to see the animals residing in the substantial Earth zone, particularly as he could expect to see many species that had already become extinct by the advent of the twenty-first century. Without doubt that amounted to a considerable tally given the propensity of humanity to eradicate the treasure trove of its fellow creatures. The dedication of the Princess and her people in transferring representative examples of fauna and flora before their demise deserved unconditional recognition and gratitude for their virtuous efforts, without which the effects of the ongoing catastrophe would have been far worse.

Alfred stood patiently on a narrow dirt track that led towards the entrance into the nature reserve some twenty metres away. There a gate in the force field was marked by a mildly opaque green haze. Kriosta and the Princess were chatting with two of the staff just outside the main door of the smallish headquarters building. It was about eleven o'clock in the morning, and the warmth of the blazing sun, plus the sight of an almost cloudless blue sky, could not help but induce a broad smile on the young lad's face. It felt very pleasant, and part of him wished that his mother could also have been present to enjoy the sensation rather than being stuck with the cool drizzle of the English autumn.

He was tempted to take off his shirt and do some proper sunbathing, which would have been a rare experience for him, but the party of aliens duly ceased their chatting and began to amble over in his direction. It did not take long before he felt one of Kriosta's heavy paws resting on his right shoulder, and one of the Martian lady's much daintier hands on his left shoulder.

"Are you ready young man?" asked the Princess. "I think you are going to enjoy this, and perhaps be rather amazed as well. Some of our residents may well knock your socks off."

"Actually, I really am very excited. And before we start may I just thank you and your colleagues, on behalf of my own race, for all your hard work in saving so many species that otherwise would have been completely lost."

"Thank you, Alfred, that is much appreciated. I must admit, coming from a world where all life died out a very long time ago, I was only too glad to have been involved with the project."

"Well for my part you are most welcome to live with us on Earth, you have certainly earned that right. I am not sure that all humans would be so welcoming, but I would like to think that the vast majority would."

Kriosta removed his left paw from his ward's shoulder and adjusted his shoulder bag slightly before taking out what looked a little like a television remote control handset. He pointed this at the entrance to the nature reserve, and the green haze began to oscillate in intensity. This was to make it clear that at this point the force field had temporarily been switched off to allow access.

"Shall we go inside?" invited the princess.

"Yes please, replied Alfred eagerly before rushing off towards the entrance, then stopping just before the flashing colour that marked its location. His impatience to go through was tempered by uncertainty regarding the force field and fear of getting a jolt from it. He cautiously waited for the others to catch up with him. His experienced tutor had no such qualms and confidently walked through to the interior without hesitation, after which he turned around and stared back at his pupil with a look of mild disapproval at the earthling's apparent wimpishness.

Alfred tried to regain some credibility by quickly shuffling through, albeit with his eyes closed, to join his friend. The Princess walked nonchalantly across the boundary with her usual elegance.

The two conservation officials did not cross over, and it became clear that they would not be accompanying the three visitors. One of them did however contribute something that would assist his visitors' trek around the park. He too pulled out a remote-control handset, but on this occasion pointed it in the direction of the reception building. A few seconds later, a fast-moving object that resembled a giant aluminium baking tray sped around the corner of the building into view and headed for the park entrance, where it came to an abrupt halt just inside. It was a larger and more robust version of the peculiar wafer-thin transport system that he had encountered inside the Historical Ministry during his visit to the Time Telescope.

"Jump on Alfred," instructed the princess. "This will take us to our first destination, which is a Nature Reserve Centre. There I will introduce you to a very important member of the conservation team who has dedicated his life to helping preserve endangered species from all over the galaxy. Come on Kriosta, you too."

Both the male members of the expedition quickly complied with the request to hop onboard. Alfred's natural instinct was to sit down since it seemed a more stable travelling position. The other two remained standing though, and he had learnt by now that what seemed natural on Earth was often completely wrong in these far-flung places. As the tray began to move off and gather speed, sure enough he could feel some invisible force holding him firmly in place in apparent defiance of Sir Isaac Newton's famous Laws of Motion.

Looking around him the immediate area was quite flat and plain, and covered in a short grass, almost as far as he could see. Further ahead in the direction that they were travelling, quite quickly now, were some low-lying sandy hills obscuring what lay beyond.

Alfred glanced over towards the Princess, and could not help but admire her smiling beauty as her golden locks flowed almost horizontally in the streamline of the onrushing air.

# Chapter Twenty-Six

The route they took eventually twisted for a while through the sandy dunes, necessitating a much gentler pace, until the tray finally slowed to a complete stop just in front of their first destination. Marlena stepped off, and the other two followed her cue.

The Nature Study Centre was largely concealed within a low artificial hill topped by a well-maintained grass covering. The only external sign of its existence, apart from a door marking the main entrance, was a ten-foot-high radio mast. This arrangement was optimal for its purpose. The two lower levels contained a significant number of different rooms with a variety of useful functions, including a kitchen and dining room, communications equipment, medical facilities and study areas. The top floor was split into two halves. The side nearest to the entrance contained a number of ensuite bedrooms, while the farther side contained some rooms with large screen monitors fed by numerous television cameras positioned throughout this part of the reserve. Along the far extremity of the upper floor was a wide viewing gallery with big weatherproof windows and a single glass door leading out onto a large balcony with a few round tables plus chairs scattered about. The main entrance was discretely sunk into the base of the hill and approached by a sweeping path that provided a very gentle gradient down from the long flat plain and subsequent dunes that formed the initial section of the park. It transpired that there were several of the covert structures dotted around the reserve.

A staff member met them just inside the entrance and took them straight up to one of the tables situated on the balcony, where he invited them to sit down. There they were able to enjoy the sun and the wonderful view that the location afforded. The Princess sat in between Alfred and Kriosta, whilst on an adjacent table they were joined by the person in charge of the conservation program, a very short male called Trelis. He was barely any taller than the child from

Earth even though he was clearly of a mature age. He was almost bald and sported a longish grey beard, along with extremely bushy grey eyebrows, and he wore a short sleeved brown tunic with almost knee length sturdy brown boots. He kindly promised to give his guests a quick tour of the facility, but first wanted to get them some refreshments, and also allow them to get a real picture of what the reserve contained and how extensive it was. It looked enormous, and yet what they could see was but a small glimpse of its true size.

Nearest to the study centre was an area that resembled savannah areas of parts of the continent of Africa that Alfred had seen on television in some nature documentaries, notably those narrated by one of his heroes, Sir David Attenborough. The youngster wondered what the great man would have made of this place if only he too could have visited it. Secretly he wished that such a trip could be possible, since the knight of the realm would without doubt have been as spellbound with the place as Alfred was.

About a mile away to the left was the shore of a gigantic lake that dominated that aspect of the vista. Its waters extended to the distant horizon, with a flat, calm surface at present untroubled by any winds.

Beyond the savannah the terrain became populated more and more by bushes and sporadic trees until this met the foothills of a substantial mountain range, becoming progressively higher with increasing distance, the tallest peak of which rose to perhaps a thousand metres.

The far right-hand side of the scene was bordered by the start of a thick forest whose trees also increased in size the further away they got so that it gave the impression of forming the sloping roof of some unbelievably large green building.

"How are you enjoying the view of the park, Master Alfred?" asked Trelis in a surprisingly deep voice for someone of his conservative physical stature, and with an air of great pride in the impressive nature reserve.

"Breath-taking, sir. Just stunning. It is so wonderful to be here. I admit that I can think of a few very good people on Earth who really deserve this thrill a lot more than I do."

"I understand why you say that as we are certainly aware of such committed naturalists on your own world, but we are very pleased to have you here. I am glad that you like and appreciate it so much."

The Princess, who was presently sitting wearing an expensive looking pair of sunglasses that she had brought with her from Earth and pulled out from her bag, looked in the sunshine like some gorgeous, ultra-glamorous Hollywood film star. She had been here before, yet was clearly just as happy as the novice schoolboy with the chance to enjoy the smorgasbord of natural delights on offer, at least judging by the broad smile on her face. Her golden hair seemed to positively shimmer in the bright yellow rays of the massive sun that warmed this part of the galaxy.

There were far more animals visible on the savannah than Alfred had noticed on the initial plain. They reinforced the illusion of this zone having been copied from Africa since the majority were very familiar and must have been imported from Earth at some point in time. Maybe an uncharitable argument could be made along the lines that this constituted some unethical form of poaching, if not a blatant act of theft. Personally, Alfred could in no way put such an interpretation on what had happened. This was principally a conservation planet designed to preserve the countless species that inhabited the galaxy, and given the rate that his fellow humans were decimating their own natural creatures he was very grateful that this place existed to help mitigate that problem.

The species that he recognised included zebras, with their unmistakable black and white stripes, along with antelope, wildebeest, giraffes, and even a herd of elephants performing their ablutions at a sizeable watering hole towards the centre of the open grassland. It was impossible to count how many individuals there were, but all told it could not have been less than a thousand, maybe a lot more than that. What was particularly interesting was the presence of a couple of species that the young earthling most definitely did not recognise. One of them stood out like a sore thumb as it was bright red. The animal was about the size of a cow, but with shorter and stockier legs, and a more pronounced length of neck that led to a somewhat small head. But it was the garish colour that stood out as the most outstanding difference to anything he had seen before.

The other unfamiliar species that Alfred could pick out, while nowhere near as distinctive as the red "cows", and also physically smaller, were rather odd creatures that looked vaguely like elongated greyhounds. There torsos were very slim and long and coated in a short sandy coloured fur. Their legs seemed to be mismatched; the two front legs were tall and slender like a gazelle's, whilst the two hind legs were considerably shorter, thick set, and very muscular, more like what a powerful jaguar from South America might have. It had a disproportionally large head and jaws with a substantial nose and small ears. Perhaps the strangest thing was that it had the appearance of being some sort of carnivorous hunter, yet the several examples on show were wandering around quite nonchalantly without sparking any obvious anxiety amongst the herbivorous grazing population.

On that point there was no sign of any other potential predators, no trace of lions or any other large cats. It raised quite a few questions about how this miniature ecosystem operated.

"It is great to see all these animals enjoying what seems to be a peaceful and idyllic life here, sir. Most of them seem to have come from Earth. Would I be correct in thinking that?"

Trelis nodded whilst taking a sip from a tumbler of juice. He lowered the vessel and thought for a moment before putting it on the round table that the quartet were sitting around. "You are quite right. This area was set up to allow us to bring several earth grassland species to live and breed here. We focus on those that are considered endangered even by your own people, although we include less endangered species to provide a balanced mix that more closely resembles the source location. The most important natural treasure from your planet in this zone are several types of rhinoceros, however you can't actually see any at the moment since most are currently elsewhere undergoing routine check-ups. There are a few white rhinos further towards the mountains in the bushier terrain, but they are fairly hidden just now."

"I could not help noticing a couple of species that I certainly do not ever recall seeing back home, or maybe I should say on television back home because I have never been anywhere near Africa. Those bright red animals are definitely new to me."

Trelis laughed briefly. "Yes, they are definitely not from Earth. On the other hand, their natural environment is remarkably similar to this and so they are more than happy to exist here. I suppose you have also noticed the other type of what you would call extra-terrestrial animal."

"Yes indeed. That peculiar, well, I am not sure how to describe it, but that thing with the really, really long body."

"Trelis could not help laughing again. "Peculiar is a very subjective adjective, but yes, I can understand why they would look so unusual to you. They are actually very nice creatures, very gentle and friendly."

"Not carnivorous then?"

"Goodness no."

"Seriously? They look a bit scary to me. Maybe more than just a bit."

"Trust me, you can go up to them and stroke them without any fear whatsoever. Their staple diet is root vegetables, ground nuts and fruit. They are very skilled at picking off low hanging fruit from trees, and also quite adept at digging with their back legs to unearth food. Their powerful jaws are built for cracking open the shells of the nuts they find. In theory they could give someone an extremely nasty bite, but I have never heard of that actually happening."

"And the red cow like things with the long necks?"

"Equally comfortable at grazing from both grasses and the leaves of trees and bushes. You can see how the long neck is useful for the latter. The red colour is to ward off predators on their original world, of which there were many. In the natural world, bright colours are employed as a warning that they are dangerous to any carnivores who might otherwise be tempted to try and take a chunk out of them. In this case the flesh layer just beneath the skin has evolved to become extremely toxic if eaten, so they are not actually dangerous to touch on the surface. Again, they are quite friendly creatures to those not intent on gobbling them up."

Alfred squinted towards the distance, but there was no sign of the white rhinos. It was nevertheless the best news he had heard in a long time that the magnificent creatures were being preserved by the people running the nature reserve. He could not help feeling more than a little ashamed that their intervention was so necessary due to the disgraceful poaching of the indigenous population back on earth. The ignorance, heartlessness, and greed of those responsible was beyond comprehension. What a contrast with the caring aliens he had met. He then remembered that there were a huge number of humans who in fact were doing tremendous work, even risking their own lives, to try and stop the poaching. That made him feel slightly better.

"Sir, I am very grateful for the work that you are all doing here. There are a huge number of different species on Earth. More than I can even imagine. It would seem almost impossible to bring every species here. How many do you actually have? And there was one thing I was particularly wondering – how long have you been doing this? Do you have animals here that no longer exist back home?"

Trelis did not answer that very good question straightaway. It seemed to especially catch the Princess's attention because she sat up straight and took off her sunglasses. She looked seriously towards Trelis who returned her stern gaze. Even Kriosta seemed a bit fazed by the question as he turned from enjoying the view to give his pupil a concerned glance.

Alfred was a little surprised, wondering whether he had said something to offend the trio of adult aliens. It was not the most pleasant of feelings to see such close acquaintances, particularly Marlena and his tutor, apparently upset. He sensed that he had overstepped the mark of what he was allowed to know. In mitigation, he had no idea at any given time what the appropriate boundaries were, although this certainly appeared to be one of them.

"I am sorry, did I ask something that I should not have asked? I didn't mean to cause offence."

The Princess put her sunglasses down and folded her arms on the table, then smiled to try and reassure him. "Please, don't worry about it. It's not your fault. We have a duty to be careful about what you can and cannot be told. At least at this stage of your education. You are both young and from Earth. That necessarily means that we have to restrict the information we give you, for our benefit and yours. It is not that we do not trust you, but we have to be strict about it. As you gain more experience and get older then we can tell you more things than we dare to now."

Trelis took another sip of juice before adding some further clarification. "As you are already aware, the situation on Earth is extremely serious and a very sensitive subject for lots of races throughout the galaxy. Please do not worry that you have offended us, and I feel confident that you understand the general situation and why we need to be so careful. To answer your question as far as I can, we split the conservation project into two separate halves. We have a large number of species that actively live here, but we also have a bank that contains embryonic matter in suspended animation along with detailed DNA profiles. That vastly increases our bio-storage capacity. The bit we can't discuss involves species that are already extinct on Earth as we speak. Please just accept that for now.

"Of course. And please accept my sincerest apologies for asking too many questions."

"That is not necessary," interjected the Princess. "Feel free to ask whatever questions you want. Remember though that you will not always get an answer, and above all understand that it might get a bit awkward at times, but we are all friends here I assure you."

"Thank you, your Highness. If only my own race were as friendly as everyone out here has been to me."

Alfred folded his arms on the table to mimic the Princess. He felt a bit less uncomfortable, and now even more curious about the question that he had unsuccessfully asked.

Trelis smiled and leaned over, putting his left hand on to the earthling's top forearm. "Would you like to meet one of those funny things with the really, really long bodies?"

# Chapter Twenty-Seven

It had been too good an offer to turn down, although Alfred was still not convinced that the intimidating looking animals were as safe to approach as Trelis had maintained. He realised that it was just psychological, yet fear was usually there for a good reason. If something looked scary, then in general it was probably best to give it a wide berth.

The gallery side of the Study Centre had a door on the lowest floor that led out to a footbridge that crossed a moat separating the building from the savannah zone. It was filled with water, but there was no sign of any marine life in it. The far side of the bridge was protected by an invisible force field gate, which Trelis deactivated just long enough to allow him and his three guests through and out onto the grassland.

The temperature if anything was getting even warmer, and down here there was absolutely no shade. It was bad enough risking getting skin cancer, thought Alfred, but for him just as big a danger was trying to explain to his mother how he had come to accumulate a handsome sun tan in the cold, dreary weather that seemed to forever dominate his home town. It was partially his own fault for not being sufficiently prepared and forgetting to bring any sun tan lotion. He resolved to place it on his list of top ten essentials for all future off-world trips.

The nearest animals were some antelopes, who looked inquisitively at the strangers before moving slightly further away just to be on the safe side. The tiny group engaging in the safari continued more or less side by side, with Marlena and Alfred in the middle and Kriosta and Trelis on the outside. The grass was no bowling green and required some effort to wade through in places, especially for the smallest of the visitors. The manager of the nature reserve was clearly used to walking through it and made it look effortless despite his own limited stature.

Although the Fanti, as it turned out the long-bodied creatures were called, had originally been some way off, when they spotted the visitors they came bounding quickly over to greet them. Whilst this was helpful as it meant Alfred did not have to walk so far, it made his heart miss a beat at the sight of them moving so rapidly. It was an odd way of running that they possessed, but it was certainly effective, with each enormous stride covering at least ten metres once up to full speed. The poor nervous boy was glad to have his big tutor by his side for protection; he struggled to put on a brave face, even though part of him just wanted to turn and run. If he had not been informed otherwise, it would have looked for all the world that he was the main course on the creature's menu for today. Their jaws were wide open as they sped nearer, presumably to draw in plenty of oxygen, showing off two long rows of substantial nutshell crushing teeth.

The nearest of the Fanti of course made a beeline straight for the little human and was upon him before he even had chance to scream. However, instead of sinking its fearsome dentures into his throat, the creature snaked out a long tongue, dripping with saliva, and with a single upwards stroke licked Alfred's chest and face, almost knocking him to the ground in the process.

"Oh, for goodness sake!" he cried out in disgust, but also relief at still being alive.

The Princess could not avoid laughing out loud, until, that is, she succumbed to a slobbering dose of the same medicine from another of the enthusiastically friendly animals. Alfred could not quite make out her own verbal comment, although it sounded like an uncharacteristically course phrase from one normally so regal.

Alfred pulled out a tissue and did his best to wipe the worst of the well-intentioned contamination from his head. The assailant by now had settled down somewhat and was sitting on its shorter haunches with its elongated torso sloping up to join the tall front legs, leaving its eyes almost level to the humans and staring directly into them. The tongue had returned from whence it came, and its mouth was now closed but unmistakeably smiling. Despite the assault, it was impossible not to become instantly enchanted by the playful Fanti.

"You were certainly right about them being friendly."

There were twelve of the creatures now forming an expectant semi-circle round the visiting quartet. Alfred stroked the top of the head of the one next to him, and his colleagues made an equal fuss of the other cute quadrupeds. Trelis was quite used to the attention; on the other hand Alfred was not accustomed to such affection from an animal, having never previously owned so much as a goldfish. Part of him almost hankered to have one as a pet, yet he knew that they clearly belonged out here roaming free. It was a nice feeling to see them happy in their natural environment, in the place that was their home.

After a couple of minutes of prolonged petting, Trelis gestured to the dozen Fanti with a wave of his right hand, and they merrily bounded off just as quickly as they had come.

"Did you enjoy that, Alfred?" asked the short conservationist.

"Yes, apart from getting drenched in saliva," replied the grinning schoolboy. "I shall remember to bring a plastic mac next time."

"Me too," concurred the Princess, "But they were adorable."

Kriosta made the sentiment unanimous. "Agree. Much nice."

"Very good," said Trelis, "Now I would like to take you into the edge of the forest over there, where we have some examples of a bird from Earth that I think you might like to see."

As he spoke the low flying tray suddenly came speeding into view from around the side of the Study Centre, gliding silently along before stopping adjacent to the group. The forest was within walking distance, however time was at a bit of a premium, literally so in one sense. They stepped on and soon found themselves in the shade of some medium sized trees with a thin dressing of beech like leaves. About fifty metres along on their left a couple of the bright red cow like creatures were using their long necks to good advantage by munching on the natural produce of some of the lower branches. It afforded Alfred a much closer view of the boldly coloured animals. They did not seem bothered by the presence of the onlookers, completely ignoring them and instead concentrating on their green feast.

Once more back in contact with the solid ground, Trelis led the way through several layers of the wooden columns until he paused a few feet in front of a fallen tree trunk. Without speaking he waited expectantly for something to happen.

After a few seconds, as Alfred was beginning to wonder what was going on, something small and round suddenly rose just above the top of the fallen log. A pair of curious eyes stared out from a coating of very short feathers. Satisfied that there was no danger, the rest of the body belonging to the eyes jumped confidently onto the top of the trunk. It was a bird. But not just any old bird. Its chubby body, short curved neck, small wings and bulbous beak were unmistakeable to the young earthling, who was a particular fan of the species, even though he had only ever seen one in books before.

"My goodness. I don't believe it. It is absolutely gorgeous. I mean…it's a DODO!"

# *Chapter Twenty-Eight*

"How is this possible, sir? Did you use some sort of cloning technology?"

Trelis moved up close to the ostensibly extinct bird and rubbed the back of its neck, to the obvious pleasure of the feathered descendant of the mighty Jurassic dinosaurs of earth. The Dodo emitted a commensurate shrill noise of delight and moved its head to press against the naturalist's face. It was a touching and moving demonstration of close affinity.

"No, not at all. In fact, we have never used any form of cloning for the species that we have had to rescue from the threat of extinction. I cannot really expand too much on our methods, not now anyway. Maybe in the future when you are older and more experienced. I am permitted to say how we obtained specimens of the Dodo. There was nothing magical or even very technical about it. Although most civilisations have thus far been reluctant to interfere in Earth's development, your world has been carefully monitored since well before humanity existed. Where considered appropriate and justified, particularly when impending extinction has come about directly as a result of man's own actions, then we on this conservation world have been given disposition to covertly land on Earth and remove a viable stock of the species in danger. The Dodo is a prime example of that policy."

"I should point out," interjected the Princess, "that the Martian population is heavily involved in the monitoring process, due to our local knowledge, as it were."

"Well, I can only say," declared Alfred, "that I salute everyone involved. This is just wonderful. I am once again almost speechless. Do you think it would be alright if I were to stroke it myself?"

"Of course. They are quite timid, and more than happy to try and bond with other creatures."

Alfred shuffled over and stood directly in front of the flightless bird, who stared back inquisitively at the small boy. He found himself almost choked with emotion, perhaps out of a sense of guilt on behalf of humanity, even if he personally had not been involved in the wiping out of the indigenous population. The profoundness of this moment could not be overstated. It made him hesitate, as though undeserving of the chance to touch this very much alive Dodo. It made another screeching sound, and Alfred took this as sufficient invitation to finally reach out with his right arm and place the hand on top of the bird's head. The feathers were very soft as he moved his fingers downward to stroke its back. He sat down on top of the log and the Dodo snuggled up against him.

For perhaps obvious reasons, it had been strictly forbidden for the earthling to bring along his mobile phone with its built-in camera. For a child of the twentieth century he was unusually not keen on taking so called selfies, but if there was one picture that he would have loved to have snapped then it was this one. To his surprise the Princess was thinking along the same lines, and did whip out a smartphone from her bag, utterly unable to resist the temptation.

"How come they let you bring along your mobile phone?" protested Alfred.

"Rank has its privileges. Come on, smile."

Never having considered himself photogenic, he did his best to strike an acceptable pose.

"Perfect. Let me just do one more. And…excellent."

Trelis felt obliged to dash any expectations of taking a print back to Earth. "Whilst I agree with taking a photograph, of course we cannot give you a copy for you to keep when you return to your home planet. It will make a great picture to hang on the wall at the library though."

Alfred understood, and was more than content with that arrangement.

Local time was pressing on, and the group only had an hour before they were scheduled to get back to the headquarters building ready for the return journey to the library. There were a couple of other things in the forest that Trelis wanted to show his visitors, so it made sense to do so now rather than try and rush to another zone. The conservation world was so large that it would take six months just to complete even a perfunctory tour of all the available zones and species.

The first object of interest was another bird, again from Earth, however this one was very much bigger. It had lived on its home world, on the island of Madagascar, until the mid-seventeenth century, when it had finally succumbed to the intrusion of human civilisation upon its remote lifestyle.

The visitors had been asked by Trelis to move slowly and quietly. As they crept through the thinnish undergrowth on the forest floor Alfred noticed that the affable dodo had decided to tag along with the group and was happily negotiating the shrubbery a few feet behind him. The earthling had taken a real liking to the thankfully not extinct bird and was pleased to continue to enjoy its company.

The alien conservationist did not seem bothered by its presence and was instead concentrating on searching for his next target species. Kriosta was sniffing the air with his sensitive nose and helping to guide them in the correct direction. Eventually Trelis brought everyone to a sudden stop by holding out his right arm level with the ground. He waited a moment then waved the others forward to where he was standing. After another few seconds the visitors gasped quietly as they caught sight of what they had been looking for. An enormous bird resembling a giant ostrich wandered out into a nearby clearing, immediately accompanied by a second. It was about ten feet tall to the top of its head and must have weighed as much as a decent sized horse.

"This," whispered Trelis, "is Aepyornis Maximus, colloquially known on Earth as the Elephant Bird. They are not aggressive, and their diet consists mainly of fruit so they are not carnivorous, however their sheer size makes then potentially dangerous, so we need to be quite careful."

Dangerous or not, Alfred thought they looked very scary, and unlike the affable dodo he was not inclined to go and give them a hug. One friendly peck of from their huge beaks would probably be enough to give him concussion. It was wonderful to see them though. Once again he was grateful that they had been rescued from oblivion. They were safe in this place.

The final item on Trelis's itinerary necessitated a short trip on the tray to an area of forest that was a little denser and had rather taller trees. There was no need to venture into the ranks of stout trunks as their quarry was unmistakeably visible as they rounded a curve in the edge of that part of the forest. The tray came to a halt some fifty feet from five elephant sized animals, two of which were standing tall on their hind legs and dragging the thick branches of one tree down with large powerful forearms and claws in order to munch on them.

"These are of the species Megatherium," instructed Trelis. "They existed on Earth up until ten thousand years ago, and your own naturalists more commonly refer to them as the Giant Ground Sloth. These are also herbivores, although we keep our distance to be on the safe side due to their extreme power and size. They each weigh about four tons. Early humans hunted them until the population became unsustainably small, so we had to bring them here. I'm sorry if I sound as though I am judging humans and have a bad opinion of them, because we are not here to pass judgement, our interest is purely in the preservation of endangered species. I am quite happy to leave the politics to others to deal with."

"To be honest," confided Alfred, "I am grateful to hear you say that. Unfortunately, there seems to be quite a lot of politics about what my fellow humans have been doing over the years, and whilst I fully understand the reasons for that, it is making things very difficult and stressful for me personally."

"You know," said the Princess, "that nobody attaches any personal blame to you whatsoever. On the contrary, you are highly thought of, as are a great many other human beings."

"Absolutely," agreed Trelis. "There are countless people on your planet who have worked tirelessly to try and save animals and the environment from harm, sometimes at great risk to themselves of injury or even death. I personally salute all of them."

"Thank you. That is high praise coming from you, sir."

There was a loud thud as one of the sloths finished its meal and dropped its heavy frame back onto a four-legged stance. It stared over to the humanoids still munching a large mouthful of leaves.

"Well, I guess we had better be getting the three of you back. I hope you have enjoyed your visit here."

Alfred, Marlena and Kriosta all nodded wholeheartedly, then each gave their host a brief hug.

"It is spellbinding to see all these animals," said the earthling. "I would never otherwise have had the opportunity to witness them for real on my home planet, nor the amazing ones that were indigenous to other worlds. Truly incredible."

The journey by tray back to the conservation headquarters building more or less retraced their original path, except for a small diversion that took them past an unkempt yet beautiful display of colourful wild flowers.

Upon approaching the main administrative edifice the quartet were surprised, non more so than Alfred, to see another spacecraft sitting alongside Kriosta's vessel. By contrast this one looked very sleek and futuristic, was quite a bit larger, and was distinctly saucer shaped. An absolutely perfect example of a flying saucer, a UFO that could have been plucked straight out from a dozen science fiction B-movies from the nineteen-fifties. Although he was now aware that such things did exist, this was the first occasion that the schoolboy had seen one, and it completely took his breath away. It was silver, windowless, and had a wide upside-down plate like lower section seamlessly topped by a smooth dome. There was a smaller diameter short curved plinth upon which the main body sat, still tall enough to house a door for access to the sleek machine. Standing just outside this door waiting for them were two men, one of them Grattin, the Magister of the Grand Library.

"That's strange," said the Princess, somewhat stating the obvious. "What is the Magister doing here?"

"Not seem good," added Kriosta.

"I agree. We'd better go and find out what he wants."

Trelis steered the tray to allow them to alight right beside Grattin, who looked very serious.

"Hello. I am sorry to turn up here so dramatically, but a matter has arisen that, while expected, requires more urgent attention than I had earlier predicted. Indeed, immediate attention to be blunt about it. Alfred, I must ask you and Kriosta to travel to the planet Joxavia without delay, and there meet with a senior representative of that race. We had a communication from them a few hours ago, where they were extremely insistent that we demand this of you today. We could refuse, however the consequences of doing so are at best worrisome. This is a species that is quite capable of wiping out the human race in the blink of an eye. Whilst we do not think that is likely in the short run, there is a risk of something unpleasant happening fairly quickly.

Alfred's stomach churned with anxiety. It had been a wonderful day thus far; the remainder of it promised to be far less enjoyable.

# Chapter Twenty-Nine

After leaving the Princess to hitch a lift back to the library with Grattin, Kriosta set the controls of his spaceship to reappear just short of orbit around the planet Joxavia. Like many of the exoplanets in far flung quarters of the galaxy it was considerably larger than earth, but nowhere near as pretty. The drab surface was mostly brown and black, that is, where it could be seen through a widespread covering of thick grey cloud. There seemed to be quite a few thunderstorms going on judging by countless enormous sheets of lightning flickering around its otherwise dimly lit atmosphere. The main city where they were heading for was fortunately clearly visible, aided by an intense beacon of light striking out into the depths of space to guide visitors in.

It took an entire orbit to slow down sufficiently for a safe landing. Kriosta skilfully manoeuvred the spacecraft towards the source of the pencil of illumination, a gigantic searchlight pointing vertically skywards. It was based nearby what seemed to be the main entrance of a walled conurbation that was large enough to house a considerable population, certainly many thousands.

Upon landing, they both strained their eyes for any sign of a welcoming committee, yet there did not appear to be anyone around at all. This was a little unexpected. After waiting a few minutes Alfred shrugged his shoulders and decided that perhaps they should get out and make their way over to see if anybody was actually at home. Perhaps there was a doorbell that they could press. Although not looking forward to meeting the residents, he was quite keen just to get this over with and leave as quickly as diplomacy would allow.

"It doesn't look like they are going to lay out a red carpet for us, so maybe we ought to make the first move, sir."

"Why would lay red carpet?"

"Sorry, it's just an expression. I didn't mean that they would really do that."

The phrase had whooshed well above his tutor's alien head, leaving the pilot looking very confused. In truth it was unlikely that Kriosta had ever attended a film premiere, so could probably be forgiven for not understanding.

There were three doors that gave access to what was effectively a mediaeval walled town from twelfth century England. All that was missing was a moat and drawbridge. The middle door was large enough to have driven a double decker bus through, whilst the two similar yet much smaller doors on either side were clearly designed solely for pedestrian access. They were all made from the same antique looking dark iron material and took the form of an arch. The large door was split down the centre into two equal halves, one of which swung open inwards as they approached it.

Inside, there was a road that ran in a circle around the interior face of the high wall and lead off in both directions to a variety of municipal buildings and dwellings. Immediately in front of them an additional road led a short distance to the nearest building, a substantial castle that suggested it was the residence of whoever was in charge of this grim place.

The walls of the castle were very high, about four storeys judging by a few sporadic windows located away from ground level. The edifice looked like a continuous rock face rather than being constructed from individual stone blocks. There were no ramparts along the top border, however a square tower that did have ramparts rose about twenty feet higher from a position directly above the entrance to the gothic structure.

Kriosta and Alfred walked over to this before then waiting in nervous silence in front of another enormous split gate, this time made of wood. It was nearly two minutes before finally a loud click could be heard from the barrier as the left-hand side began to swing inwards, accompanied by a loud whirring sound. There was little to be seen inside but darkness, suggesting that this wall must be pretty thick. Kriosta fumbled forward, gently clutching the boy's arm to ensure that he stayed very close.

As they shuffled inside they could at last see a glimpse of the interior of the castle on the far side of the immense stone barrier. The wall turned out to be some thirty feet wide. Anyone trying to lay siege to this place was in for a very hard time trying to make any sort of breach through which to invade the paranoidly well protected home.

Emerging back into the open, a rather unpleasant smelling space it had to be said, they could see that this new area consisted of a number of what looked like houses and barns that formed a tiny village surrounding a central building that itself formed yet another, smaller castle. There was a tall square tower jutting out from the final castle that was absolutely jet black save for a colourful emblem towards the top.

The ground was not paved but consisted of a firm surface that resembled dry but not fired clay. There was straw strewn around in places but no sign of any animals, and still not a trace of the indigenous Joxavian population. Following a brief frustrated glance at each other they continued towards what was hopefully the final obstacle to their protracted progress.

The entrance to this central keep was extremely ornate, with a border of quite gruesome dark carvings depicting creatures that were universally fearsome and almost certainly carnivorous. Some looked like dinosaurs from long ago in Earth's past, but most looked like nothing Alfred had ever seen before even in history books. The material of the border seemed to be an almost black wood such as ebony.

The door itself, imposing and impregnable, was made up of vertical planks of a lighter wood with a bronze like metal bracing along the bottom, middle and top. The wood was weathered and dented in places as though vain attempts to batter through had been made at some point. It was rectangular in shape, with the now characteristic split in the middle and stout hinges at either side. There were no obvious locks or handles, but a heavy ring knocker sat about six feet off the ground, too high for the small earthling to use.

As the two visitors contemplated the entrance they shared another worried look at each other. It was as well that Alfred had his tutor with him at his right-hand side, because presently all he wanted to do was turn around and run as fast as his legs little legs could carry him. If the high placement of the door knocker was anything to go by then the Joxavians were no midgets.

Kriosta looked apprehensive and similarly reluctant to proceed, however there was no choice in the matter. He carefully reached and lifted the stout ring with his powerful right paw before slowly rapping it three times on the solid wood. The loud sound that emanated rang out and echoed around the stone walled courtyard. Kriosta then shuffled back as it was not clear whether the doors opened inwards or outwards. It turned out to be the former, with both enormous slabs of wood creaking apart steadily into the building.

Beyond a single step that defined the boundary between inside and outside, there was a short corridor that terminated in an opening that led through to what seemed to be a very large room. There were no lights in the gloomy corridor that instead drew its meagre illumination from the flickering of what was presumably one or more fires situated within the cavernous interior space. There was still no sign or sound of life as yet. This only added to the tension as the anxious earthling was forced to let his imagination run wild as to what the infamous Joxavians looked like in the flesh, and whether they would prove to be as frightening as their reputation would have it.

The only way now was forward, so Kriosta put his left paw behind his ward's back to encourage him to enter as they stepped inside and inched slowly onwards towards the expectant large room.

The floor was made up of a patchwork of hard grey slate tiles of greatly varying sizes all cemented into a continuous uneven surface. Kriosta's wide bare feet made little sound as he padded along, whilst Alfred's hard plastic heels struck the slate with a harsh click that resonated along the passage.

The visitors were a metre from emerging from the corridor when a brief fearful wailing sound from the large room made them both jump and stop for a moment. They tried their best not to tremble over what had caused the sound, which resembled the cry of some large and none too friendly trespasser-eating animal. Whatever it was, they could only hope that it was on the end of a very strong chain.

Knowing there was no choice but to carry on, Alfred took a deep breath and strode forward into the interior chamber. His tutor, caught out by the demonstration of resigned boldness, hurried to join him.

The room transpired to be very long, maintaining a constant width but rising in height towards the far end. The nearer zone closely matched the footprint of the large swimming pool at the youngster's school. The additional height further along allowed the far end to house an upper level reached by an impressively wide straight staircase made of stone, which had a narrower red carpet climbing its centre that also stretched out halfway towards the newcomers. Despite his fear Alfred could not help appreciating the irony that it turned out that there was a red carpet laid out for them. There remained no sign of life, including any potential emitter of the horrible noise.

Most of the uncovered floor was made up of the same irregular size slabs as those of the corridor, however just before where the carpet began there was a ten-foot diameter circle created from an uncharacteristically ostentatious, colourful and elaborate mosaic of tiny ceramic tiles. It would not have been out of place in an ancient roman villa back on Earth. The image it formed was not very clear from their current vantage point.

The stone walls of the lower floor were generally covered by multiple drapes of a heavy fabric of varying earthy colours, interspersed with occasional sheets of brighter colours that had printed upon them symbols that, if they meant anything to the locals, were nonetheless incomprehensible to the strangers.

Also attached to the walls, jutting out from them by about a metre, were large burning torches evenly spaced every ten metres or so, and it was these that had been responsible for the flickering illumination they had observed earlier. The ceiling formed a featureless shallow stone arch over the room.

With nobody apparently around to greet them, and in the absence of further instructions, they gravitated towards the mosaic that turned out to be a quite detailed and accurate plan of the city they were currently standing in. A shiny golden plate in the middle had an inscription on it written in whatever passed for the native language. The image was artistically beautiful, and the pair could not help staring at it and admiring it for a few moments.

"Ascend the stairs."

A loud, deeply spoken order echoed around the harsh walls as the startled visitors looked around in all directions, but still there was no one else to be seen. They reluctantly skirted round the mosaic, not wishing to step on it in case that was deemed disrespectful, then started to walk towards the steps to the upper level. They both hesitated before transferring onto the spotlessly clean red carpet, glancing down at their respective clay caked shoes and paws. Again, in an attempt to avoid causing offence they chose to walk along the side of the carpet rather than upon it.

Kriosta looked more serious and apprehensive than Alfred had ever seen before, save perhaps for their joint encounters with the terrifying hypercats. The longer fiery hairs of the fur on his head had a tendency to fluff up in such situations, Alfred had observed, accentuating his nervous disposition. In the boy's case it was his stomach that invariably seemed to display the most glaring signs of distress, and right now it felt quite nauseous. He took hold of his tutor's left arm as they headed towards the foot of the stairs.

As they reached the first step they simultaneously became aware of a faintly pungent odour that seemed to be cascading down from the upper level, although there was no visible trace of any obvious fumes. Kriosta's much more sensitive nose twitched at the smell as though it was causing him some discomfort.

The steps were each conveniently low enough in height so that even the smaller of the visitors could climb them without stretching, which was perhaps as well since a rush of adrenalin had made the youngsters legs resemble the consistency of jelly, making the ascent that much more taxing.

The tension as they reached the uppermost inflexions of the stairs was almost unbearable for the ten-year-old earthling, and this became even more intense as his much taller tutor became the first to be able to peer over the top of the stone ridge, suddenly stopping cold in his tracks. Kriosta's lower jaw dropped open and his eyes bulged widely.

"What can you see?" squeaked Alfred timidly. There was no reply, so Alfred forced his trembling legs up another five of the steps to gain enough height so that he too could peek over, letting go of the security of the alien's arm in the process. He too froze at the sight of what lay in the flame lit scene that now lay before the stunned visitors.

# Chapter Thirty

The two startled outsiders had not been able to see anything of the upper level from their original vantage point down in the large open space of the lower floor. Now they could clearly see all the details; ahead there were two new sets of stairs some ten metres ahead on either side, each much shorter with only six steps, leading to two separate long corridors that were poorly lit and disappeared into gloominess. The rest of the upper level was flat save for a small raised area with an enormous throne like chair at its centre. On the wall behind this was a dark blue velvet drape, with a large flickering torch set half way up on both side walls.

Sitting in the chair, and also standing up flanking it, were three gigantic figures, fairly human looking except for their size and a distinctly Neanderthal appearance. Joxavians. Each seven-foot-tall, muscular in the extreme, and weighing goodness knew what, but surely above thirty stone apiece. The seated figure appeared older and portlier, whilst the two apparently standing guard over him had the chiselled, fatless features of much younger adults. The senior official was clad in simple, austere grey robes with a sleeveless over vest of a gold threaded fabric decorated with red embroidered symbols. The guards showed a lot more flesh, wearing a metallic blue raiment over their torsos that fell to a few inches above their knees. Beneath this was a short sleeve blue tunic that only just jutted out from the bottom of the raiment. Their only other attire were tall silver boots that reached fifteen inches up their shins. They also sported a thick mane of hair along with a full beard. By contrast the sitting alien was clean shaven and completely bald.

The guards were devoid of any sign of weapons. Frankly they looked as though they would not need any, and would be quite capable of dispatching an adversary with a single blow of their enormous bony fists. Assuming, that is, they had not scared their opponents to death first.

The sight of the Joxavians alone would have sufficed as reason enough for the visitors to have become frozen to the spot with trepidation. In fact, the principle reason for their horrified transfixation was something else. On the floor to the outer sides of both guards were two gigantic, well, things, as they seemed to defy any other meaningful description. About half their mass was taken up with the head, mostly teeth to be honest. Big sharp teeth the size of daggers. There was a smallish abdomen and four legs, two comparatively small hind legs plus two far more substantial forelegs that were tipped with frightening large claws. They were not creatures built for high speed, but heaven help any victims who were caught by them, as the end would have been swift and unbelievably gruesome.

Both the things were currently sitting back silently on their haunches, however neither of the visitors had any doubt that it was they who had been responsible for the banshee like wails that they had heard earlier. They had small eyes that stared right through the soles of the invited intruders.

Both Alfred and Kriosta were satisfied that they were plenty close enough to be able to conduct any necessary conversation, so the top step was as far as they were going. The seated elder beckoned them nearer with his right hand, but the visitors were not budging, and just simultaneously shook their worried heads.

"You do not need to be afraid", boomed the deep voice of the senior Joxavian. "You have my personal guarantee that you will not be harmed".

The words, spoken in surprisingly clear English, may have been designed to settle the nerves of the travellers, but there was a great doubt as to whether the gruesome staring animals understood or agreed with the sentiment. There function could hardly have been that of a cuddly companion. These were not pets, they were surely only there to intimidate.

"We are pleased to meet you," croaked Alfred diplomatically, though it did not sound particularly convincing. "I am grateful for your guarantee, but it is really hard not to be afraid, sir."

The official's bloodshot eyes squinted from beneath prominent brows; they were not designed for looking amicable, but he did at least seem to be trying his best to display some sympathy for the human representative's predicament.

"I believe that you know why we have requested your presence here, earthling. It is to give you notice, on behalf of all members of your species, of our intention to bring an end to the destruction of the natural elements of your planet by humans. We have been more than tolerant in the hope that things might improve, yet instead things have continued to get worse. This must change quickly, and if we must enforce such a change ourselves then so be it."

The speech came as no surprise yet was still painful to listen too.

"One thing that is unusual about Earth and the human race is the speed that your species and its civilisation has developed at. You went from being a small, rural, agrarian society to a huge, predominantly urban industrial society within the space of two hundred of your earth years. But worst of all, and by far the biggest problem, is that the number of human beings increased relatively slowly over time until your so called twentieth century, when the population growth rate suddenly began to increase exponentially. It literally took tens of thousands of years for your race to expand to one billion individuals, yet now the growth rate has rocketed to an extra billion every decade. Think about that young earthling. An extra billion every ten years instead of every ten thousand years. Nowhere in the galaxy has there ever been a similar situation amongst species that have developed into a state of intellect sufficient to master communications and advanced technology. Nowhere. Only very primitive creatures and organisms have displayed that characteristic of population explosion beyond any capacity of their natural environment to sustain and cope with such growth. For example, rats and viruses on your own planet. Do you know what our own experts consider the optimum human population size to be? One hundred million. That is little more than just one percent of what it currently stands at."

Alfred continued to remain silent, ashen faced and unable to speak, let alone give a cogent response to the emotionally delivered critique from the alien official, who had just compared the human race to a plague of rats or a deadly disease.

"Let me ask you, Master Alfred, before I give my own answer. And I apologise unreservedly for putting you in the position of having to give an opinion, because I know how unfair that is. What do you think should happen? Should your species be allowed to continue to destroy the natural environment of the planet Earth, or should something happen to put an end to the madness?"

To Alfred's great surprise, he found that there was part of him that actually wanted to give a reply to this impossible question. Perhaps it was as a result of feeling angry at the monstrously unfair position he had found himself in, or perhaps it was just the absolute craziness of the whole situation, but somehow, from somewhere, he found his voice.

"I will give my personal opinion, sir. I am not qualified to speak for humanity. I am just a young schoolboy. But it is my planet as much as anybody's, so for myself I tell you that I agree that such destruction should not be allowed to continue. And I also tell you that I am not alone in thinking that. There are many, many humans who are just as distraught about what has been happening, and who would like to do something to help. But they feel utterly powerless to do anything. So, if you are about to suggest wiping out my species then I beg you not to, because there is so much good amongst my people, even if there is also so much bad. Surely you can help us, rather than use your overwhelming power to destroy us."

Kriosta put his paw on the boy's shoulder, and simply whispered, "Well said, Master Alfred."

The sitting Joxavian unexpectedly rose to his feet. For a moment Alfred feared that the massive body before him had become angered at his response. Just as unexpectedly the frightening alien's face suddenly broke into a smile. "I agree with your escort. Well said. You are very brave."

Moving two paces nearer, the official reverted to his more serious demeanour. "My opinion is that we should give the human race one further chance to right the wrong themselves. Before we intervene directly, and forcefully, we shall give the Galactic Council the opportunity to provide some help, to more covertly influence the actions of humanity, and significantly change the course of development on Earth. We now formally declare this to you, as ambassador for your people; stop the abuse and exploitation of your natural treasures, and stop it with all haste. We will not wait long to witness major improvements. Consider your race officially warned, and officially on notice."

Alfred stared up at the stern visage filling most of his field of view, his own face now red with a combination of shame and worry. There was a further unmistakable emotion present though, that of relief at humanity having been given a stay of execution, however temporary."

The Joxavian returned to his seat, lowering himself with care as though concerned his enormous weight might shatter the solid piece of furniture.

The schoolboy managed to compose himself enough to ask if there was anything else to discuss at present, or whether it would be alright to leave and go back to Kriosta's spaceship now. The official confirmed this to be the case.

"You are free to leave now. I genuinely hope that it will not turn out to be necessary for us to take any action, and I wish all concerned well in your mission to change things sufficiently to appease us. Go in peace, Master Alfred."

The visitors stepped carefully backwards a few paces, then turned around to head as quickly as dignity would allow back to Kriosta's spaceship. Once outside the central building there ensued a cascade of lightening flashes accompanied by ground shaking roars of thunder, yet thankfully no deluge of rain to dampen their already soggy spirits. This was a depressing world, but perhaps that went some way to explaining why the Joxavians had taken such exception to what was taking place on the comparative Garden of Eden that the Earth represented.

The journey back to the library did not take long. The journey ahead for Alfred in his task to help redeem his fellow humans would doubtless be far more arduous.

# *Chapter Thirty-One*

Winter weather was a brand-new experience for Kriosta, at least with respect to snow. Strictly speaking it was the final days of autumn, but the final season of the calendar year had decided to put in an early appearance. The alien had been in cold environments before; from the safety of the cockpit of his spaceship he had been on the surface of celestial bodies that were far colder than even the artic regions of Earth. Snow though was a meteorological phenomenon that he had surprisingly hitherto never come across. He quickly came to the conclusion that he was not a fan of the soft frozen state of water. Many humans, for example those from the Nordic countries such as Miss Larsson's home nation of Sweden, seemed to have a considerable fascination for snow, regarding it as pretty and even fun. Kriosta, on the other hand, just saw it as an inconvenience. As his big furry feet ploughed through a thick carpet of the stuff on the way to the Princess's house he glanced down and sideways at his heavily garbed pupil doing his own best to make headway. Then he glanced backwards at the unusual tracks he was making compared to the many trails already left by shoe clad human feet. It left him worried, if truth be told. They looked more like the footprints of a polar bear, not a species normally to be found frequenting the sidewalks of that particular relatively temperate English town.

Fortunately, the snow was not falling just at the moment, and there was an almost complete absence of any wind. It was very quiet, and distinctly chilly. The red door of number four was a welcome sight as they slowly approached it.

Alfred was also less than enthusiastic about powdered snow. Additionally, he was still feeling frustrated that he had not been afforded the opportunity to go inside the shiny flying saucer that he had all too briefly encountered before their forced diversion to the planet Joxavia. It had just looked so astonishingly and perfectly futuristic; every dubious corny old science fiction movie that he had ever seen simply cried out for him to have taken a ride in it. He loved his tutor's less than sleek spacecraft, but that was different. He could only hope and look forward to getting another chance at being a passenger in the genuine, classical UFO.

As in their previous visit they were initially greeted by one of the handsome young Martian attendants who escorted them through to the lounge.

"Hello again, your Highness."

"Hello Alfred. Welcome back to Earth. I gather that your trip to Joxavia was not quite as bad as you feared it might be. You are a very brave young man for having agreed to travel there."

"Thank you, although I didn't feel as though I had any option but to go, so maybe I am not that brave. Given the choice, I would definitely not have visited such a frightening place. However, as you said, it was not quite as bad as I had feared. The Joxavians were scary, but they were not as hostile as their fierce reputation implied. Frankly, they put forward a quite logical and reasonable argument as to why they are so angry with the human race, or rather what the human race has been doing to its own planet."

The Princess sat down in one of the two armchairs of her cosily furnished living room, then gestured for her visitors to make themselves comfortable on the sofa. "I agree, they are not a naturally aggressive people. Instead they basically have a philosophy that revolves around the premise that it is better to operate from a position of military strength, and also to use that strength robustly if they think it is morally justified to do so. The main thing that separates the Joxavians from the other major galactic civilisations is their readiness to intervene. They are not without support in that attitude from many quarters for their willingness to take action. Who is to say whether they are right or wrong?"

There had been one very important question that Alfred had known he would have to ask at some point. He realised now that the time to ask it had clearly arrived. "Your Highness, what is your own opinion? Should they go ahead and take measures against humanity to protect the Earth?"

The Princess did not reply straightaway, just sitting with a pensive expression. Finally, she did speak, however she obviously judged it appropriate to turn the uncomfortable question back upon the young Earthling. "Perhaps it is more important that you yourself pronounce whether you think that they should intervene or not."

Now it was Alfred's turn to avoid an immediate reply. He lowered his head and sat in agonised thought, trapped between his loyalty to his own species and the extremely deep concern that he felt for the natural world, with its immense variety of animals and plants. This seemed to be the crunch point that recent events had all been leading to.

"You know, your Highness, that I think that whatever answer I give will be the wrong one. If I agree that the Joxavians should intervene, perhaps even killing large numbers of people, then that makes me sound like a monster. On the other hand, I am devastated about what is happening to the natural world and really want the destruction to stop right now. So, what answer can I possibly give?"

The Princess nodded. "I feel exactly as you do. Neither is acceptable. That is why we must devote ourselves, to the very best of all our abilities, to taking advantage of the Joxavian's offer to let us try to find a third way."

Alfred too nodded. "But what exactly is that third way. Do you know how we should proceed from here?"

"No. But I have some suggestions."

There was no elaboration, forcing Alfred to prompt for some. "Which are?"

Marlena stood up and wandered over to look at a renewed cascade of snow falling outside the room's large bay window. Alfred decided to rise and join her.

"I think, young man, that we are in for a cold winter. Would you like to come with me to somewhere much, much colder? I would feel happier continuing this discussion there."

"I suppose so. If you think that is best." The idea did not really appeal to the schoolboy, but he assumed his host must have a good reason for the strange request. "Where did you have in mind? Not the Antarctic, I hope."

"Dear me no. I'm thinking of somewhere even colder than that." The Princess turned and put both arms onto Alfred's shoulders. "How would you like to come to Mars with me?"

# Chapter Thirty-Two

The last time that Alfred had felt quite like this was the occasion of the school trip to the planetarium. The three main differences this time were the people boarding the coach, the type of coach, and the attraction that they were all heading for.

The travellers this time were not his classmates but an assortment of Martians, about forty in total, some of whom may have looked only ten years older than his fellow Lime Lane Primary school friends but whose age in reality was on average several hundred years. The Princess, currently towards the front of the queue as they waited to board, was two thousand years old, not even middle aged yet by her extraordinary extra-terrestrial standards.

The coach itself was, somewhat surprisingly, not as different from an earth bus as might have been expected. There were no wheels, yet apart from that the resemblance was uncanny. It was slightly longer and wider than a typical luxury earth coach but no taller. There were luggage compartments accessible from the outside located below where the passengers sat, and upfront a small cabin where the driver, or in this case pilot, was sitting waiting patiently. Just behind this was the entrance, with a robust door providing the necessary tight seal against the vacuum of space.

The destination was not the planetarium, with its spectacular electronic show, but this time the real thing. A journey through the heavens to the red planet itself, Mars, currently fifty million miles away. About nine months distant using earth technology, though just over seven hours away in this deceptively terrestrial looking Martian vehicle. It appeared much sleeker and more modern than Kriosta's rustic machine, but the furry alien's spaceship was almost infinitely faster with its astonishing quantum-based engine. Alfred had no idea how the bus before him worked, only that its top speed was about one tenth of the speed of light, and that they would be going about half that speed on average today.

Alfred could not at all get his brain around those sorts of numbers, and feared that his head might explode if he so much as tried. His limited experience of interplanetary travel, and particularly the technology used, had led him to the conclusion that the best thing to do was just enjoy the ride and not ask too many questions for now. That was probably the only approach that would allow him to retain a vestige of sanity, or at least what sanity had been defined as before he had come across the Galactic Wide Web.

He was half way towards the back of the queue, but noticed the Princess beckoning him to join her as she was just about to board. He felt a little uncomfortable about jumping the queue, after all he was British, but felt he had no choice but to scamper forward to join her since she had invited him to do so.

"Are you excited about the trip?" she asked, gently pressing him in front and up the three stairs that gave access to the interior.

"Extremely, but I'm also very nervous."

"Well, that's only to be expected. But it really is quite a comfortable journey. Very similar to taking a long coach journey here on Earth, except that there are no motorway service stations to stop off at, or any laybys with bushes for that matter. You will be relieved to hear that we have more than adequate facilities on board, including a couple of loos!"

"Thank goodness for that. I don't think I could wait seven hours before, well, having to pay a visit."

There is also a small kitchen at the back, so you will be well fed and watered along the way. There are no formal hostesses on this flight, so we all take it in turns to help out."

"Even a Royal Princess?"

"Most definitely. If we ever get properly established back on Mars then maybe I can be waited on hand and foot, but until then I am happy to muck in and do my bit."

Once they were both inside the Princess ushered her young charge five rows back and gestured to him to take the window seat to his left, so that they were on the right-hand side when facing forwards. Each row was divided by the aisle into two spacious pairs with ample width and legroom, as well as very plush sprung seats with soft fabric and large headrests. Definitely first class, not that he had ever experienced what first class air travel was like before. He shuffled about a little to get his position just right and then sighed, more than content with the level of comfort on offer. The Princess likewise seemed very pleased, although in her case it was not just the high standard of the travel arrangements that was putting an obvious smile on her face. Rather, it was most especially the prospect of returning, albeit briefly, to her home planet. She leaned over for a moment to help her fellow traveller put on a lap belt, rather like that used on a commercial aeroplane, before doing up her own.

"Don't worry, it is a very gentle journey, but take-off and landing can be a little bit bumpy as we go through the atmosphere. It is not so bad on Mars as the atmosphere is much thinner."

"I hope that I don't feel airsick."

"I am sure that you will be fine, however let me know if you are not. I guess that is easy for me to say, as I have done this journey so many times before. In fact, it is a pity they do not give out Airmiles like on a normal airline. Fifty million Airmiles would get me a few free flights back on Earth, I suspect."

The space bus was starting to rapidly fill up as the other travellers eagerly took their own seats. They were an interesting assortment of sizes, shapes and apparent ages. Just across from Alfred and Marlena were a young-looking man and woman, whilst behind them were two older looking men, one tall and stout, whilst the other was rather shorter but still also a little stout. The larger gentleman seemed to be talking in a Birmingham accent, whilst the smaller spoke with an obvious Scottish accent. They seemed like a very affable pair.

A couple of minutes more and everyone seemed to be correctly set in their places. The main door hissed as it swung shut with a reassuringly tight thud. Alfred was suffering from his usual minor signs of trembling due to an adrenalin rush as he waited in anticipation for the flight to begin. The interior lights dimmed and changed from white to dark blue as an expectant hush fell upon the occupants of the packed cabin. Suddenly, without any noticeable sound of an engine being fired into life, the bus lurched upwards several feet. As it then began to inch forward, Alfred could just see the doors of the warehouse building that acted as a hanger for the spaceship begin to slide apart, until the gap was wide enough to allow the vehicle to make its exit out into the darkness of the night. It moved slowly forward until it was completely outside, then there was a distinct jolt as the coach began to rise vertically very rapidly, as though everyone was sat in the most express of express elevators. It was more unpleasant than Alfred was anticipating, however at least it did not last long as the orthogonal ascent was soon replaced with a more gentle forward acceleration, and after that by a relatively shallow climb that steepened gradually to an angle of about twenty degrees. This lasted for about fifteen minutes until the myriad of separate lights Alfred could see down below had merged into a more amorphous glow, indicating that they were now well above the altitude that any airliner had ever achieved. At that point the vehicle appeared to level off before shooting forward quickly enough to press the young lad's small body very firmly back into the thankfully well-padded seat.

Achieving orbit was something that Alfred was beginning to understand by now to be at least half the battle in space travel. Though hardly a seasoned astronaut, he felt he was starting to get the hang of the basics. Orbit was all about speed rather than height, despite the two being inextricably linked. The great Russian rocket scientist Tsiolkovsky had realised this at the start of the twentieth century and formally expressed the notion in his famous rocket equation. At any given altitude the spacecraft needed to achieve a specific orbital velocity, after which it would stay going around and around a planet indefinitely. The vessel was still falling under the influence of gravity, but its forward motion was quick enough that its trajectory would miss the ground below. Anyone inside the spacecraft would fall at this same rate and therefore would effectively feel weightless.

After a further five minutes the silent acceleration ceased, to be replaced for a few seconds by a queasy feeling in the stomach until the artificial gravity system, similar to that in Kriosta's machine, cut in to restore personal stability. From memory Alfred knew this meant their speed was now about eighteen thousand miles an hour, yet there was little to betray this other than the obvious gentle rotation of the planet Earth beneath them. Elsewhere lay the deepest black of space, punctuated everywhere by the sharp pinpricks of billions upon billions of stars. It was a breathless sight that one could never tire of or cease to wonder at.

Marlena may have been far more used to the experience than her young charge, yet she still appeared transfixed by the view of both the heavens and her beautiful adopted world. The lights in the coach subsequently switched to a brighter and paler blue, which prompted her to release her lap belt and stand up.

"I drew the short straw for the tea rota so am on first. Would you like tea or coffee?"

"Oh, er, I'll have some coffee please. Milk, no sugar, please."

"I remember".

A low volume murmuring rose up amongst the other travellers as the Princess headed towards the kitchen at the rear. By the time she returned, pushing a surprisingly low-tech wooden hostess trolley, complete with cups, saucers, beverage urns, a milk jug, and some opened packets of biscuits, the Earth was beginning to rapidly recede into the distance as their long journey to the red planet commenced in earnest.

# *Chapter Thirty-Three*

"We will be landing in about ten minutes. If you look out of your window you should shortly see something very interesting."

Marlena lent over Alfred so that their faces were almost touching, and they both peered out of the thankfully sturdy window into the very thin Martian atmosphere. The coach was drifting slowly across the planet's rock-strewn surface at an altitude of one hundred metres.

"We have to be careful when we pass over it not to let it catch a glimpse of us, but it is NASA's Mars Curiosity Rover."

"You're kidding."

"No, absolutely not. It really is the Rover. Actually, it is becoming an increasing risk, as the Earth's exploration probes become better and more sophisticated, for us to move around Mars without being spotted. We have to continuously track these probes very carefully from our subterranean base."

"I see your point. It would be embarrassing to say the least if the scientists back home caught sight of a flying coach full of Martians cruising past. That would certainly give the conspiracy theorists something to talk about".

The princess giggled. "Embarrassing? I think it would go a long way beyond just embarrassing." She thought for a moment and then started to look more serious. "It is interesting that you say back home. Of course, when it comes down to it, Mars is really my home. On the other hand, I have lived most of my life on your planet, so in that sense it is also my home too. It is a strange feeling sometimes."

"You are most welcome to live with us your Highness. Most welcome. Me casa su casa!"

Marlene smiled, recognising the Spanish phrase to mean 'my house is your house'.

"Mochas gracias, signor," she replied fluently, reminding the youngster that she had lived in many countries and learnt many languages during her very long tenure on Earth.

After another minute of scrutiny, Alfred pointed his finger and let out a yelp. "Over there, Marlena. There it is. Wow, incredible. It really is the Mars Rover."

He could not resist pulling out his mobile phone and snapping a picture, even though he knew he could never show it to any of his friends. The Martians had been surprisingly relaxed about him bringing along the now ubiquitous device, in contrast to the much stricter authorities at the Grand Library, however he had been obliged to promise on his honour that he would be very responsible regarding its use. Photographing the Rover was admittedly stretching his freedom to take a snap, but at least it was earth technology, and if necessary it could be passed off as a photoshopped picture if the worst came to the worst.

The coach driver banked slightly to the left in order to alter direction, suggesting that he had deliberately made a small detour to allow his only human passenger to see the robotic explorer. The new heading pointed towards a very large mountain a few miles away. It had a flattish top, indicating that it was almost certainly a volcano, one of the many left over from the planet's more active distant past. It rapidly grew larger as the travellers sped quickly towards the base. With about a mile to go the spacecraft began to rise quickly whilst maintaining a level pitch, so that it eventually ended up hovering just over the wide crater at the summit.

To his astonishment Alfred noticed that the sunken floor of the crater was moving, with a part of it sliding to one side to reveal a rectangular aperture slightly larger than the footprint of the bus. A subdued light emerged vertically, and the driver manoeuvred until the coach was directly above it before slowly descending inside the top of the mountain. Thirty seconds later a very gentle jolt announced that they had arrived at their destination and their long trip was over.

The young boy felt Marlena's hand on his left shoulder as he looked out of the window at the mined out artificial interior of the volcano.

"It will take a few minutes to repressurise the landing chamber, and then we can go and get something to eat before I take you to your quarters. We have given you your own little bedsit on the minus third level."

"Minus third?" Alfred was puzzled by the negative floor level, but quickly realised that since they had landed on top of the volcano then it was actually quite logical that everything would be referenced from the highest level downwards. "Oh, I get it. Ha, that's quite sensible really. Minus third level, of course."

The Princess realised that what was normal for her was less natural for the newcomer to the red planet. "I guess we are a little upside down here. Don't worry, I'm sure a clever chap like you will get used to it before long. Anyway, the room is not very big, but it is yours permanently, so you are effectively the very first human to have a home on Mars. Welcome to our world."

"Oh my goodness." Alfred was genuinely taken aback by what the Princess had just said. There was no way he felt that he deserved such an accolade, and his head dropped down onto his chest in a subconscious show of humility. "I don't know what to say. I mean, thank you so much, but I am not worthy of this honour. I'm really not."

He put his head in his hands and was close to tears. It had suddenly once again become overwhelming, too much for the ordinary ten-year-old to cope with.

The sensitive princess realised how distressing the situation now was so pulled the youngster towards her to comfort and reassure him. She was not too surprised at his reaction given the enormity of the occasion, coupled with the unfamiliarity of the surroundings.

"Of course you deserve it," she whispered. There is as much good in you as I have seen in any human being, and there are plenty of very good humans. We are all very happy, and also feel extremely privileged, to have you here with us."

Alfred felt a bit better, but still could not bring himself to accept that he was deserving of any special recognition for what to him was simple circumstance. It had been pure chance that had led him to be here, if one discounted any form of divine intervention or other greater conscious power at work. There was no special talent possessed by the common boy that had served to engineer his passage to this extraordinary location. He did appreciate what a great privilege it was anyway, and gratefully accepted it on behalf of everyone belonging to his species.

There followed a slight sense of anti-climax, as they all patiently waited for the thin Martian atmosphere to be slowly augmented with additional oxygen and nitrogen. In the meantime, Alfred cast a curious eye over the spacious airlock. The now closed roof was encrusted on the inside with a large number of small bulbs that bathed the internal space with more than enough light, which bounced off the pure white circular walls to make the spaceport look clinical and rather harshly lit. There was little to absorb the bouncing photons and add any contrast or colour. Around the perimeter were several cabinets attached to the wall, but what they contained was for now hidden behind their closed doors and drawers. Perhaps tools and spacesuits were likely occupants.

The only other notable feature, close to the wall directly on the right-hand side of the coach as currently oriented, was a wide bench with two chairs plus a bank of monitors stretching across the rear of the workspace. There was no indication of anything being presently switched on.

After ten more minutes the pure white scene became contaminated with a flood of refreshing green light to indicate that the airlock was now fully pressurised and safe for both human and Martians to walk out into. The front door of the bus hissed into action and swung open, and the driver got up then alighted, followed by the other passengers as they filed out.

The Princess waited until last before standing up and pulling her bag down from the overhead shelf where she had stowed it some fifty million miles and seven hours ago. That was about the same time it would have taken an airliner to cross the Atlantic from New York to London. She passed Alfred's bag down to him as he joined her in the aisle, and then the pair shuffled out to where the others were standing.

There was quite a bit of stretching of cramped limbs going on amongst the weary crowd, and the solitary human joined them in trying to get the blood flowing properly again by raising his hands above his head and wiggling his fingers. His two-thousand-year-old royal escort seemed a lot fresher and more supple; she helpfully massaged his shoulders for a few seconds.

Presently there was a loud whirring sound from a point straight in front of the long space vehicle and the wall there began to part as two large doors slid aside in opposite directions to reveal a short corridor leading to what seemed to be two open lifts at the far end. The assembled throng took the cue and began to stroll towards the elevators, and in a very orderly manner entered each six at a time. It took about a minute for the vertical cars to complete their errand of ferrying each set of arrivals to their respective floors and then ascend back to the top level again. After three rounds of short trips there were only eight people left waiting to be transported. As the lifts came back into view for the final time the left-hand car was not empty this time but contained five young looking men clad in white jumpsuits. They seemed to be some sort of technicians. They nonchalantly walked past the visitors towards the workbench, where two of them sat down and began to fiddle with the instrumentation surrounding the monitors. The other three opened up some of the lockers and took out various tools. Before Alfred could track their activities further the Princess put her arm behind his back and with a very gentle shove encouraged him to move into the right-hand lift.

"Come on, we'll go down to the restaurant on level minus five and get you something to eat, as I am sure you must be hungry by now."

"Oh, yes, that would be nice. Thank you."

The last group of guests distributed themselves evenly in the two lifts and the doors closed, the floor slowly falling away for twenty seconds. Once it came to rest the doors swished quietly apart to reveal another corridor, this time a bit longer. There were large windows on the left side that allowed a good view of what was clearly a largish dining area with places for about a hundred people sitting around ten communal tables. It looked simple yet still quite inviting, with colourful walls and comfortable looking chairs, and somewhat unexpectedly some fancy candelabras and other silverware atop the eating surfaces.

"This is nice," commented Alfred as he walked along looking sideways. "I feel quite peckish, and actually I think I must have lost some weight as I feel very light, so I could probably do with scoffing a few calories."

The Princess laughed as they reached the open entrance to the restaurant. "I'm sorry to disappoint you but you haven't lost any weight at all. Remember, we are on Mars, and the gravity here is only just over half of what it is on Earth."

Alfred slapped his right palm to his forehead as he suddenly remembered. "Ah, how stupid of me. Of course, I had almost forgotten. Oh dear. Mind you, this is one way of dieting without having to starve yourself."

The princess continued to giggle. "Never mind, you are slim and healthy anyway, so enjoy the food and drink."

"I'm sure that I shall. Where are all the other people from the bus? Are they not having anything to eat?" There were indeed only a handful of other diners present at the moment.

"Most of them have gone straight to their rooms. We Martians don't tend to have huge appetites, and I am sure they will pop along when they do get hungry."

There were four people already eating at another table, but instead of joining them the Princess and four other of the travellers sat down along one side of a vacant table, inviting the earthling to sit at the end with the royal lady immediately to his left.

Two of the others were women and two were men. The girls, for they barely looked more than teenagers, looked similar enough to possibly be sisters. The two men looked to be in their fifties, although as the human had come to learn their real age was a complete lottery. One was small but the other was much taller. They both smiled politely but did not speak.

After a light meal of thick soup and bread, the youngster began to show obvious symptoms of fatigue, partly because of the long bus ride, and partly due to the adrenalin that had been coursing through his veins for some time, along with the unusual environmental conditions.

The Princess took him along to his new quarters, the small bedsit that he had been allocated. It was about the same size as his compact bedroom back in Lime Lane, a little longer and narrower with a lower ceiling. There was a bed built into the left wall as viewed from the doorway, whilst to the right was a short sofa, also built into the wall, and beyond that a small refreshment area with a sink and some appliances that had clearly been purchased back on earth and transported here. Most important of these was an electric kettle for making a cup of tea. Usefully there was also a microwave cooker. Underneath, as the Princess helpfully demonstrated, there was a small fridge stocked with a few basic groceries such as milk and fruit. At the far end was an open door leading into an ensuite bathroom. Although restricted in size it looked immaculate and comprehensively kitted out.

"It's perfect." Alfred placed his bag atop the white duvet of the single bed and then joined it, his short legs dangling freely above the bedsit's green carpet. "Its not home, and I am starting to really miss my mum, as usual, but it is still very nice. As are you, your highness."

Marlena ruffled his short, dark hair with her right hand. "Don't worry, we will have you back home very soon. Tomorrow will be a difficult day as we try to hammer out some sort of plan, but for now you just relax and get some sleep. I understand that this is not your real home, any more than the Earth is my true home, but from now on it will always be here for you. Sleep tight, Alfred."

# Chapter Thirty-Four

"I can't believe the view. I know that it must be real, I know that I am awake, but I still can't bring myself to believe it."

Alfred was sitting in a very comfortable chair that might have been borrowed from a chief executive's office back on Earth. It was oversized for his diminutive body, yet he felt completely at ease in it. The chair in turn was seated in a prime location at the centre of a large viewing gallery that looked out over a panoramic vista of the Martian surface from the high vantage point near the summit of the extinct volcano.

There were a score of similar chairs in the extra-terrestrial conservatory, with Marlena currently the only other occupant, sitting relaxed in an adjacent seat to her young guest. She had an aura of contentment staring at the barren scenery of her home world

"I sometimes feel the same way," she replied without turning to face him. "I just feel so grateful to be able to come and visit here every so often. As they say on Earth, there's no place like home."

"Do you consider this to be your home more than you do the planet where you have actually lived most of your life?"

The Princess now did turn to face Alfred, swivelling the chair in order to do so. "Yes, very much so. I can't help it. I love the Earth, truly, but you must realise that I am one hundred percent Martian. This is my real home, however uninhabitable it may be at the moment. It is in my DNA. Just like the salmon has an irresistible urge to eventually return to the river from where it was spawned. I hope you can understand."

"Absolutely. Personally, I think that is wonderful. I just wish that your world could be turned back into the paradise that by all accounts it used to be before the great natural disaster that it suffered. I hope that can be made to happen in the future."

"Well, there are plans to take some steps along that road. Have you come across the word terraforming before?"

"Yes, in a couple of science fiction movies. One of them was called Aliens. My mum was not very keen on me watching it alone, so she sat through it with me, which was good of her, but I think it rather freaked her out. It was very scary. Frankly, I am very pleased that the only aliens that I myself have come across have thankfully not been all that scary. With the possible exception of the Joxavians, that is, but even they were not that bad once you got to know them. Mind you, there were the Hypercats. To be honest they were terrifying. All in all, though, I am pleased to report that I really like most of the aliens that I have had the great privilege of meeting. Especially Kriosta and, well, you your Highness."

The Princess's cheeks seemed to flush at the compliment. She stretched out her left hand, as she was sitting immediately to Alfred's right, and he responded by taking a gentle hold of it with his own right hand for a few seconds.

"That means a lot to me. Thank you. By the way, I have also seen that film and I agree, it was very scary."

Alfred grinned and retrieved his hand before taking on a more serious expression. "Marlena, there is one question that I have been meaning to ask you for a while, but please don't answer it if it makes you at all uncomfortable. I hope I am not being really rude or inconsiderate in asking it."

The Princess raised her eyebrows in surprise and uncertainty at the nature of the inquiry. "My goodness, I wonder what it is that you think that I might be reluctant to answer. I think perhaps it is best if you just go ahead and spit it out."

Alfred became unsure as to whether he should proceed with the question. After hesitating for a few seconds, he decided that he now had to proceed with it. "How did you come to be a Princess, your Highness?"

Marlena must have been expecting such a question at some point, although her failure to answer straightaway confirmed his suspicions that it was indeed a sensitive subject to broach. She glanced out towards the Martian landscape before returning her gaze to Alfred and finally replying. "I guess to answer that requires me to emphasise that I am not human, and instead belong to a species that is remarkably similar to your own, yet distinctly different in certain key ways. I feel such an affinity and closeness with human beings that it makes it especially difficult when I have to draw attention to how different I and my fellow Martians are. The fact that I am a Princess also emphasises the fact that I am actually unique with respect to my own race too."

She stood up and walked a few paces forward until her face was almost touching the transparent barrier that divided interior from exterior. This was obviously not the easiest conversation to hold for the lady from Mars. "As you know, we live for much longer timespans than humans do, typically ten times as long. Well, my lifespan is far greater than that. I guess the closest analogy I can think of is the queen bee in a bee hive, or the queen in an ant colony. They are physically different from the rest of the colony, being much larger, and they also have a special role to play. Well, in the same way I am physically somewhat different, even though in my case I do not look so, and I too have a special role to play."

Marlena turned around to look back towards Alfred again, and winced nervously, paradoxically looking as human as Alfred had ever seen her look. "It is not so easy for me to talk about the exact differences, perhaps we can return to that topic at a later time."

"Please, I am so sorry if I made you feel awkward. I am very grateful to you for saying what you already have. That makes things a bit clearer. Thank you so much, your Highness."

At that point the door to the room slid open and a line of ten Martians filed calmly in, taking their places in half of the remaining unoccupied chairs. The Princess sat back down too, and once everyone had settled she brushed both edges of her beautiful blonde hair back behind her shoulders before formally confirming why everyone had gathered there.

"Thank you all for coming. We are here to discuss the situation regarding the potential intervention by the Joxavian race into the future path of the human race on Earth, and in particular what measures we ourselves can take to alleviate the potential devastation that might cause to the dominant species. As you all know by now, we are fortunate to have a representative of the human race with us, Master Alfred Smith."

The naturally shy schoolboy was becoming more used to being the centre of attention, but he still could not avoid blushing as he just silently nodded in acknowledgement to the introduction.

"I spoke with the President of the Galactic Council yesterday, and he briefed me on their own recent meeting with the Joxavian emperor. The outcome was a little better than I had feared. At least there was some form of consensus. The council managed to get the Joxavians to agree to take no independent action against humanity at this time, which was not easy because as you know they are very angry about what has happened on Earth. The end result is that it has bought everybody a little more time, but only on the proviso that the council puts in place a plan to take some sort of direct action themselves, and within a relatively short timescale. The details of the plan have yet to be thrashed out, however they confirmed, Alfred, that they expect the Martian contingent on your planet to play a key part. In addition, everyone feels that you also will have to be quite heavily involved."

"I was already aware of that. On the other hand, I am just a ten-year-old schoolboy. It is difficult to know what I can do to help"

The Princess was clearly concerned about what lay ahead for her and the rest of her race, but she was also acutely aware of the indigenous earthling's own difficulties. "I know that, young man, but for good or bad, right now you are all we have available as far as humans go. Personally, I think that there is no human being that I would rather have by my side in this mission than you, despite your age and inexperience. There is a goodness in you that overrides your youth, and a wisdom that belies your tender years. The Council, Grafton and Kriosta all agree with that sentiment. The responsibility will be mainly mine, so do not worry about it too much. Your best help is absolutely all we ask, and I believe that you will be glad to help us. What do you say? Would you like to join my team?"

Alfred was not sure how he felt, apart from huge trepidation, however there was only one answer that he was ever going to give. "Your Highness, it would be my greatest honour to be part of your team."

# Chapter Thirty-Five

"This is not going to be easy. We will get a lot of support from the Council and the Library, but it is really down to us, I mean those of us actually residing on Earth, to make a difference."

The atmosphere in the viewing gallery, now temporary conference room, was not very upbeat. Alfred would have preferred it if Grattin and Kriosta were present, however they were deliberately absent for precisely the reason that the Princess had just stated. This meeting was exclusively for those who lived on the Blue Planet. They were the locals and therefore best placed to carry out whatever plan was eventually settled upon.

The young earthling arguably had the most vested interest since it was his race that had caused the problem, and it was his race who would be paying the biggest price if the project to stop the blight of the natural world failed. It was the Martian's though, led by their wonderful prospective queen, who in practice would carry the bulk of the effort that would be needed. Alfred's young age contrasted starkly with the ages of all his allies in this noble and absolutely essential venture, none of whom were below a century of years. He had no choice but to bow to their maturity, expertise and cumulative wisdom. That would not stop him from doing his very best to contribute in whatever way he could.

"Perhaps we should recognise straightaway the most significant aspect of any likely plan." It was the most elderly looking alien in the room who had spoken up, making use of all his obvious years of learning. Despite his appearance he was considerably younger than Marlena at only eight hundred years old. That was well into old age for a normal Martian, whose typical lifespan was a little over a millennium.

"You mean the fact that we will have to involve some human beings, probably making them aware of our presence," replied the Princess.

"Yes. It goes without saying that the fewer who are exposed the better. We will have to think long and hard about exactly how to do it, and most importantly who to contact."

"You are, as always, most wise Calton, and I thank you for your counsel. I agree completely with what you say. We should also acknowledge that whoever we do talk with to elicit their help, we will unavoidably be placing them in a potentially dangerous situation. We therefore have a responsibility towards them too, and should take that into account when deciding who is appropriate to choose with a view to assisting us."

There was a brief pause in the discussion that Alfred decided to take advantage of. He had been thinking of an idea for a couple of days now and realised that this was the time to suggest it to the others.

"I don't know if this is a useful name to put forward or not, but I know someone back on Earth who might be a possible candidate. His name is Doctor Brewster. He is a physicist and astronomer working at the university next to my home town. Although not a politician or a person with great influence, he is a good man, at least I think so. He knows a lot about space, by human standards. In fact, his favourite subject, would you believe, is the planet Mars.

There was a ripple of mirth that went around the room, temporarily breaking the immense tension that inevitably existed regarding such a monumentally important matter. The Princess looked amused too. She also looked both puzzled and intrigued.

"I don't think I remember you mentioning him to me previously, Alfred. Obviously, I do not know him, however it is an interesting suggestion. Perhaps we should find out more about this human academic. Actually, make that we must find out more about him. If he sounds promising, do you think you will be able to find a way to introduce us? Whatever he seems to be on paper, naturally I am going to need to meet your good doctor in person, to assess his character and suitability for myself."

"I would love to take you to see Dr Brewster, although I assume you mean as a human being rather than a Martian."

"Absolutely correct. Just as a twenty-nine-year-old human lady, please."

"You will have to help me come up with some sort of cover story, your Highness. I can't think of how to do it, at least not at the moment."

"Well, it will take a little while for us to check him out, so that gives us some time to devise a suitable ruse. I guess it is not as easy as it sounds. Why would a ten-year-old schoolboy know an older woman like me? Wait a minute. How about I am somebody working as a science journalist in America, and you have read one of my articles on the internet and sent me a question? We exchanged a few emails where you mentioned Dr Brewster in one of them. I said that I would be visiting England soon and thought it might be a good idea to arrange an interview with him."

"Brilliant. What a great idea. Are you any good at doing an American accent?"

"Are you kidding me? I am very good at accents. Remember that I have been around for a while, including quite a few years spent in the United States. In fact, I was there before the revolution, when it was still part of the British Empire. Used to live in Boston. You know, where they had the infamous tea party!"

"My goodness. Sorry, I keep forgetting. You still look so young."

"You are too kind, young man. Calton, could you please make a note regarding getting in touch with Doctor Brewster. We can organise the details when we return to Earth."

There was another pause in the proceedings when two more people turned up, this time accompanied by a refreshment trolley. The coffee and biscuits were just what Alfred needed to keep going.

"Your Highness," he asked, scoffing a favourite dunked custard cream, "It is great if we can get some of my fellow humans onboard, but what do we then do to change things for the better, at least enough to satisfy the Joxavians?"

Marlena had been coming to that anyway, however seemed reluctant to say what needed to be said. She shared Alfred's enthusiasm for custard creams and took advantage of this to delay the inevitable for a few more seconds. It was the less sweet toothed Calton who decided to force the issue.

"It is blindingly obvious that, however unpalatable, we must admit that whatever we do it will not be enough unless we are willing to address the P word"

Alfred did not immediately get what Calton was driving at. "The P word?"

Calton did not reply but stared at Marlena. She put down her cup and wiped her mouth clean of some stray calorific residue.

"He means P for population. It is not a word you ever here terrestrial politicians using, and with good reason. Nobody ever got voted in by telling people that there are just too many of them."

"I see. And I understand," said Alfred, still clutching onto his own cup. "When you say population, you are referring to the fact that the number of humans is already too large, I presume. As I see it, there are then two main questions; firstly, is it enough to simply stop the population size getting bigger, or must it be reduced; secondly, exactly what measures do you think will be needed to control it?"

"Thank you for being so blunt," said Calton. "I agree completely with your two key questions."

Everyone's eyes were now firmly directed towards their royal Chairperson, who folded her arms on the table, resting upon them without responding straight away. In the room full of uncomfortable people, she now appeared visibly the most stressed.

Eventually she lowered her gaze and just stated, honestly, "I really don't know. I suppose that deep down I do know, but it is such a difficult subject to have to even discuss, never mind actually deal with." She stopped for a few more seconds, this time twirling her hair with her right hand in deep thought. "Gentlemen, the question of numbers is probably moot at the moment. It is a certainty that whatever the required figure, the growth in the size of the human population is not suddenly going to miraculously come to a stop by itself, so positive measures will be needed in some shape and form. We can do nothing but accept that as a fact. So, we should be focussing our efforts on how to do this as compassionately as possible. Burying our heads in the sand like an ostrich is not an option."

All eyes now shifted back in the direction of the sole human attendee, searching for his reaction to the very blatant statement by his host. Alfred knew that what the Princess had just said was an irrefutable declaration of the reality of the situation. The truth of the matter was that there existed a plethora of educated people on his own planet who agreed with the premise that population growth had gotten wildly out of hand over the course of the last century.

"Your Highness, like a great many humans I agree that the expansion of our population is the main reason for causing problems with nature and the environment. And I agree that something needed to be done about, it even without the threat from the Joxavians. So, as you rightly point out, the issue is all about how exactly population control can be done whilst causing the least suffering. I am sure that everyone here wants to avoid any harm coming to people already alive."

To the youngster's surprise, the small assembled throng broke out into a spontaneous gentle round of applause. He nodded in acknowledgement.

"Thank you, Alfred. OK then, let us be very direct and discuss the specifics of what can be done, and what we feel, well, perhaps not happy to do, but at least willing to do. There is, in my opinion, one other issue equally as important as population growth, and inextricably linked to it. That is deforestation. The greatest biodiversity exists in places such as the Amazon jungle, along with the forests in countries such as Borneo. These are being encroached upon and destroyed on literally an industrial scale. The obscenest aspect of this is that much of it is done solely for financial gain and profit. The people and corporations responsible have displayed a wholesale disregard for the fauna and flora that they are so ruthlessly eradicating. Whilst I have some understanding for the difficulties of governments controlling their population growth, there can be no excuse for the heartless decimation of these natural habitats. I am not averse to a more proactive level of interference in order to help counter the excesses of deforestation."

There were no objections from any of the species in the room to that part of the manifesto.

For the following hour the meeting was conducted with a professional, detached, almost cold demeanour that resulted from the unimaginable importance of what was being discussed. It could not have been done any other way, as the presence of emotion would have made the task nigh on impossible. Alfred caught on about this strategy early on and did his best to hide his own feelings.

Eventually, with every person present having made some contribution, Calton summarised on a single side of paper the acceptable options that they had come up with. He then said them out loud so that the team were all clear regarding them.

"We agree that our immediate primary goal is to initially limit the size of the human race to around the current level, with the added long-term goal of getting it down to below five billion. This figure could be increased in the future once the species possesses the ability to travel to and peacefully settle upon other planets. With the obvious exception of Mars, of course." Alfred could not help smiling at that qualification. "This goal must be achieved without resort to killing any humans, rather by control, preferably consensual, of the natural birth rate."

Everyone nodded in agreement. The Princess then took over the summation. "We are also agreed that this must be done without humanity being aware of alien intervention with their development, either by us or any other alien races, ultimately the Joxavians. The key phrase therefore is covert intervention."

"The specific methods to be used are fourfold," resumed Canton. "Firstly, by way of the creation of a political movement to raise awareness of the various problems, and also persuade indigenous governments to acknowledge them and take measures to control both population size and the destruction of natural habitats. That is not going to be easy, and I am dubious as to how effective it will be, given previous indifference by the majority of politicians. Secondly, assuming it becomes necessary, we need to put more forceful pressure on international bodies and individual governments to act. We shall therefore create a bogus terrorist faction to both raise awareness and also intimidate them into action. I stress that we will avoid actually harming people, merely employ the threat of such harm. Thirdly, and only if absolutely unavoidable, we will have to consider using biological means to slow down natural birth rates. That puts us into difficult moral territory. However, we should remember what the alternative is if we are not successful. We should always remember that."

The Princess waited a few seconds for the message so far to sink in before again taking over with the statement. "Fourthly, we do not have so much time to achieve our goal. There is no set time limit, but the Joxavians must at least clearly be able to see that progress is happening. Consequently, we must quickly involve a select number of human beings in this program to assist us. A very select group, men and women who above all we can trust, and who we feel would be fully committed to the project and understand completely the need for it. It is inescapable that we may have to tell them, to some extent, who we are, but otherwise information should be given on a strictly need to know basis."

After another brief pause, and with everyone clearly fatigued by the intense discussion, Marlena brought the meeting to a formal close. "Thank you everyone for your contributions. I am very grateful and satisfied with the plan. Let us finish there. We have a lot of work to do on some of the details, but I am convinced that we have a decent strategy in place. Those of us returning to Earth on this occasion will set off tomorrow. In the meantime, enjoy your stay on our beloved home world. Ashannee!"

Unexpectedly the other Martians all stood up in unison and called out boldly, "Ashannee!" They then began to filter out. Soon once more there was just Alfred and the Princess left as the sole occupants of the viewing gallery. Outside the light was beginning to fade with the approach of the Martian night, as the very distant sun lowered itself gently towards the horizon.

"I was a bit stumped at the end there, your Highness. What does Ashannee mean?"

The Princess had thought nothing about it, but now realised that her guest from Earth would certainly not have come across the word before. "Congratulations. You have just learnt your first word of the native Martian language. It means, well, it doesn't really mean anything to be honest. It is just a word we use as a collective affirmation of approval and solidarity."

"You have your own language?"

Marlena looked quite indignant. "Of course. Why wouldn't we? After all, we are Martians, you know."

# *Chapter Thirty-Six*

It felt like an eternity since Alfred had last seen the front door of his house at number fifty-three Lime Lane. He felt so exhausted by what had happened in the intervening days that he could barely slide his key into the lock. The journey over millions of miles and thousands of years was already taking on the unreality of a dream; for now he was just glad to be back once again. It had been the most amazing experience, but way too much for him, and he simply craved the completely earthbound sanctuary of his mother's arms and then his bedroom. Tomorrow, he could get back to school. His soul was desperate for a few days of normality.

The door opened, and he limped through into the lounge. Sarah was sitting watching television, but jumped to her feet upon spotting him, holding her arms wide open. He needed no further encouragement to stagger over and gratefully throw his own arms around her torso.

"Welcome home young man. Did you have a nice time?"

"Time? Yes, time. Very nice,"

The question seemed such a simple one, but his wonderful parent could have no appreciation of how complicated the inquiry was in the context of what he had been through. The whole concept of time for him had irrevocably changed. His first experience of deviation from normal Earth time had been for just a few brief seconds during his first test of the small time dilator that he had rented, amidst his altercation with the nefarious Billy Foyle in the schoolyard at his primary school. Following recent events, he was now considerably more skewed from his earthbound peers' temporal frame of reference. No wonder the Magister had cautioned him about how careful they needed to be about what he did, and how much it affected his personal time profile. Even the trip by coach to Mars had necessitated some adjustments because of the speed they had travelling at and the resultant effects due to Einstein's Special

Theory of Relativity. It was going to prove quite a headache keeping track of it all in the future, or indeed the past.

The present at least was crystal clear. Some home cooked food, a bit of television, a hot bath, and a good night's sleep under the duvet of his own bed.

Alfred could forget about his new-found responsibilities for a few days and get back to being an ordinary schoolboy. Next week he would go and visit the wonderful Princess once more, and together with his new-found Martian friends begin the awesome task of trying to make the world a better place, and to save it from the wrath of the Joxavians. The one part of that daunting odyssey that he was definitely looking forward to was the opportunity, subject to Marlena's approval, to somehow involve Doctor Brewster in the clandestine project. He knew how important it was for humans to act for themselves before that option no longer existed. The only way then left ahead would be the nightmare of intervention by darker and far less sympathetic forces from a distant alien world.

## About the Author

John R Parker currently works as an international consultant in the space industry, having spent the vast majority of his professional career in that field. A significant amount of the hardware currently orbiting the earth was designed by him. Additionally, manned space flight is a particular area of interest and expertise.

The author is also a very keen supporter of environmental issues and nature in general. He has previously been a runner up in the ICI Scientific Essay Competition and received a commendation in the BBC Nature Writing Competition.

Something else that is important to him is passing on learning to the younger generation. He recently undertook a teacher training course and has worked as a tutor for Mathematics and Physics students. He holds university qualifications at Bachelor and Master's Degree levels in Physics.

Printed in Great Britain
by Amazon